Tim Winton decided to be a writer when he was
ten. It seemed like a good idea at the time and
twenty-seven years later he still hasn't come up
with a better idea. He lives in Western Australia
with his wife and three kids who are all into
surfing and major headbanging. He's been called
a surfing bogan, a heavy-metal hippy and a fat old
git who writes books and refuses to grow up. All
true.

Other books for children by Tim Winton

Jesse
Lockie Leonard, Human Torpedo
The Bugalugs Bum Thief
Lockie Leonard, Legend
Blueback

lockie leonard

SCUMBUSTER

TIM WINTON

PAN
Pan Macmillan Australia

All characters in this publication are fictitious and any resemblance to real persons,
living or dead, is purely coincidental.

First published 1993 in Piper by Pan Macmillan Publishers Australia
First published 1997 in Pan by Pan Macmillan Australia Pty Limited
This Pan edition published 2003 by Pan Macmillan Australia Pty Limited
St Martins Tower, 31 Market Street, Sydney

Reprinted 1997, 1998 (twice), 1999, 2000 (twice), 2001 (twice), 2002, 2004

National Library of Australia
Cataloguing-in-Publication Data:

Winton, Tim 1960–.
Lockie Leonard, scumbuster.

ISBN 0 330 27446 5.

I. Title.

A823.3

Printed in Australia by McPherson's Printing Group

For Jesse, Harry and Alice

We are finding who we are
We can see forever

KING'S X

So you cut all the tall trees down
You poisoned the sky and the sea
You've taken what's good from the ground
But you left precious little for me

MIDNIGHT OIL

It's love that holds it all together
I just had to let you know
That it's love that's holding back the weather
And the same will let it go

KING'S X

LOCKIE LEONARD,
BLOOMIN' STUPIDO

Lockie Leonard bolted to the top of the dune and stopped dead. He dropped his board and towel without a glance. He didn't wipe the sweat from his face or the flies from his heaving chest. All he could do was breathe and look. The rumours were for real. The sea was fairly pumping.

Out in the Sound, the granite islands exploded with white spray that hung in the air like fresh washing. The water was grey as the sky and alive with huge bending swells that lined up regular as corduroy. They cracked against the headland, surged past the harbour and charged in to the

1

bay. It was demented out there.

Lockie felt the muscles twitching in his legs. He scratched his sunstreaked hair. His tan glistened with sweat. Down the beach he saw a few kids from school still dressed and sitting nervously on their boards. They looked over at Lockie, waiting to see what he would do. He was the hottest grommet in town, but no one seriously expected that even he would get in the water today. Already a couple of boats had broken moorings and come guts-up on the beach. You'd have to be loony to go out in that lot. Foaming at the mouth. A rubber-room candidate. Seriously impaired. Or at least a bit uninformed about death. This was surf movie stuff. These were the kind of waves you drew in the back of your maths book. They shuddered into the bay and peeled off thunderously, hollow and dark and evil as sewer pipes. They hissed and rumbled and moaned. Oh, Lockie heard them alright. That was the language of the hospital and the graveyard. No, you'd have to be an idiot with a head like a shoebox.

But he was still the same old Lockie, the human torpedo, the kid mothers referred to as 'that nice boy with the surfing addiction'.

Lockie stripped down to his orange speedos, pulled on his boardshorts, and grabbed his board. That's me, orright, he thought. Lockie Leonard, bloomin' stupido.

He got to the water's edge as a beautiful lull came over the bay. Me luck's changing! he thought. After a losing streak longer than the Indian-Pacific, things had turned around. He paddled out through the shorebreak in the strange calm and got out into deep water. No sweat. His luck was on the turn. First week of the summer holidays and a cyclone makes a two thousand kilometre detour down the coast and brings this! After a weird first year of high school, after losing your first and fabulous and only girlfriend and going down in flames in front of the whole school and being reduced to the level of the kind of person who sniffs bike seats for a thrill, something had to change.

Lockie felt invincible. Which was probably his second big mistake of the day. The first mistake of the day was leaving the safety of that sand dune back there where some bogan kid stood watching him. The lull was over. The new sets were coming, and suddenly Lockie couldn't see the sky anymore. The water was warm, but his blood went cold. He paddled out to sea, digging for his life. Spray lifted off the crests of the first two. Lockie paddled up hill and down dale, but he gave up when he saw what was behind.

There are times in a thirteen-year-old's life when he doesn't know whether to pack his bags or pack his dacks. Most of the time you don't get a choice so you do both at once.

The wave that came at Lockie Leonard looked like it had been riveted together by Russian welders. It was not a pretty sight. Lockie thought it might be his last. He just turned and went with it. Might as well die standing up. Kids were on their feet in the dunes. He saw their mouths open and their hands up. He was a hell of a sight from the beach – a fly speck on the side of a moving mountain. You had to wince.

He dropped down the nasty grey face with his mouth open and his eyes closed. Imagine jumping out of a plane on a lead skateboard. When he hit the bottom he was still standing. Not just standing; he was surfing! He could not believe it. What a hellrat he was.

In a long wobbly arc Lockie cut a bottom turn, feeling his hand skate across the churning face. He climbed back up and saw the great wall of the wave hollowing out, ready for him. He fell into a crouch and suddenly he was inside. He needn't have bothered crouching, though, because it was big as a two car garage in there. A two car garage with the roller-door down and the lights out.

Aaaargh!

Lockie plummeted.

He flapped like a seagull.

He pedalled like a ten-speed.

He got quickly depressed. For about a quarter of a second.

4

Then he hit the sandbar feet first and the board hit too. And bounced up. Right up. Right, right up. Oh, he felt it alright. Right in the goolies.

The crowd dispersed shaking their heads and the beach was suddenly empty.

PAIN

Eventually, slowly, horribly, Lockie washed
ashore. How did cowboys do it, jumping
off balconies right into the saddle on those
old movies? The pain was hideous. It was
like a dirty venetian blind that shut out the
rest of the world. He lay with his head on the
sand beside his board and his feet still in the
water.

'You orright?'

Lockie saw something blurry.

'Hey mate, you okay?'

Two black desert boots. A pair of grimy black

Levi 501s and a checked flannel shirt tied around the waist.

Gulp. This guy was not from a friendly tribe. A bogan. Bogans were Lockie's least favourite kind of people. They were the enemies of surfers everywhere. Three of them gave Lockie a flogging last term at the roller rink in front of every kid in town. Even his girlfriend, Vicki Streeton, had dumped him for a bogan – what else could they do to him?

'Urgh,' said Lockie.

'Eh?'

'Brrgh.'

Lockie looked up and saw the kid wore a King's X tee-shirt. Black of course. His hair was black too, and cut in a stiff dunny brush do. He had the kind of tan you only get from living underground, and his face looked like a pepperoni pizza. A bogan kid with world-beating zits, Olympic-standard pimples. This kid could represent his country in the skin problem playoffs. It took your breath away, but then Lockie's breath had checked out already.

Even though this kid was a bogan Lockie might have felt sorry for him, but he was too busy feeling sorry for himself. In the last five minutes Lockie's gonads had become tonsils. He could feel them throbbing at the back of his throat. He broke out in a sweat. Aaarrgh! He was not having fun. He cursed the cyclone, the surf, this whole crummy little country town, and his rotten luck.

'You nut yourself, mate?'

'No, I'm listening to the chemical structure of beach sand – what do you think?'

'I think you copped one in the groin, as they say. Wonder why they call it a groin?' said the bogan kid looking out at the groyne inside the headland. 'A groyne is just a pile of rubble after all.'

'Rubble. That's close.'

'You gonna stay there half in the water?'

'Only till I'm sixteen.'

The pimply bogan laughed.

'You got a sense of humour.'

'Obviously.'

'I saw you go out. You're *obviously* not a very intelligent person.'

'Obviously.'

'You're that Lockie kid, the one that Vicki Streeton dumped.'

'Obviously.'

The kid shook his head and scratched at his zits.

'Feelin' lucky, are ya?'

Lockie began to laugh; he couldn't help it.

'Yeah, I'm feelin' lucky orright.'

The bogan kid stood there a long time while Lockie writhed in pain and the light began to fade.

'Sure you don't wanna get outta the water?'

8

'Mm.'

'Dunno what you surfies see in it.'

'What's your name?' said Lockie wincing.

'Geoff Eggleston. They call me Egg.'

'You're a Metal Head?'

'I like metal music, yeah.'

'Dunno what you see in it.'

'It's getting dark, you know. Can you walk?'

'Walk? Mate, I'm just tryin' to stay alive. When's the last time you got nutted?'

'Years ago. In a cricket match. Copped one fair and square.'

'Geez, I hate cricket.'

'Me too.'

'Dunno what they see in it.'

Egg laughed and Lockie managed a smile.

Getting one in the goolies is like falling in love. It takes up most of your attention and it takes a lot of getting over. It was black dark when Lockie and Egg saw the torchlight coming down the beach.

'Lockieee?'

'That's me dad,' said Lockie. 'Stand by.'

Lockie's Dad was the local police sergeant.

He was kind of skinny and good looking. He tried to hold poetry readings in the lock-up and he confused the whole town; he just wasn't anybody's idea of a cop.

He got wet through carrying Lockie up the beach to the paddy wagon but he was like that.

9

'Snagged the wedding tackle, eh?'

'Sarge – '

'Anyway, who's this man in the King's Cross tee-shirt?'

'King's X, Sarge.'

'It's a band,' said Egg.

'Do they bite the heads off chooks?'

'No,' said Egg.

'Oh,' said the Sarge, sounding a bit disappointed.

'They just play music.'

'Sarge's into Creedence and Neil Young,' said Lockie as he was loaded into the paddy wagon.

'Sad, really, isn't it?' said Egg.

'Nothing wrong with Creedence,' said the Sarge. 'But I agree, Neil Young's a bit of a drip.'

'Why do you listen to him?' said Egg.

'Habit, son. I just got used to the little git.'

In the back of the paddy wagon that stank of vomit and those little smelly deodorant pine tree things, Lockie and Egg watched the town lights flow by.

'I didn't think bogans had brains,' said Lockie.

'Uniforms – they're all bulldust. Don't look at the uniform, look at the person.'

'Where d'you live, person?'

'Up the hill a bit. Near the Baptist Church. My old man . . . well, he's the minister.'

'Oh, mate, we both got problems!'

They laughed and laughed all the way through town and the warm rain fell in the streets and everything went steamy.

'Where to, son?' called the Sarge through the grille.

'The Baptist Church,' said Lockie. 'His dad's the minister.'

'What's your dad into then? Punk rock?'

'Barry Manilow, actually.'

The Sarge shook his head sadly and drove on.

Lockie wondered if maybe he'd made a friend. But with a bogan?

STAYING OFF
THE SUBJECT

Everyone at Lockie's place that night tried to stay off the subject of . . . well, off the subject. Lockie sat crookedly and fiddled with his chops and potato but was still in too much pain to be hungry. Mrs Leonard, who was probably the most sympathetic person on the planet (she was so sympathetic it made your hair curl; sometimes you wished she'd see the worst in people just for a change) found it hard to get the smile off her face. She patted Lockie's leg and the vibration nearly killed him. He rang like a bell.

'Oh, sorry dear, did that jangle you a bit?'

Phillip, his little brother, snorted and a chunk of mashed potato got caught up his nose.

The Sarge stuffed his face full of meat to disguise his own grin and tried not to look at anyone else.

'Come on everybody,' said Mrs Leonard. 'Eat up. Aren't you hungry, Lockie?'

'Nah. Sorry.'

'I hear the surf was really throbbing down there today.'

That was it. Not the best choice of words, but that was it. The Sarge and Phillip roared and blasted and thumped and choked. Mrs Leonard covered her mouth with her hand. Only Blob didn't notice. His little sister sat in her highchair just looking at them. All Blob did all day was fill her pants and gnaw the wallpaper, so he was safe from her.

Lockie got up from the table.

'Come on, son,' said the Sarge recovering a bit. 'We didn't mean any harm.'

'Sure,' said Lockie. 'My understanding family.'

They all looked a bit sheepish now, all except Blob who looked like she was building something nasty inside her nappy. Lockie got up and went to his room.

Lying on his bed while the others watched 'The Simpsons', Lockie thought about things. He was thirteen years old and he'd lived in Angelus for nearly a year now, but he was still lonely. It was weird being a copper's kid at the best of times, but in a little town like this it was like having 666 tattooed on your forehead. On top of that, Lockie was a city kid and no one was going to let him forget it. He was on his own.

It hadn't always been this tough. Actually the rest of the year had been a bit of a hoot. For a while there, a couple of terms back, Lockie Leonard was a total somebody. A surfing legend. A romantic goer. Vicki Streeton and him were the School Couple. Man, she was so clever and pretty. Lockie'd never been so happy in his life. He was popular; he was hot-as.

But Vicki dropped him and his life went down the dunny. He was crushed. It was worse than a whack in the nuts, that's for sure. Then school finished and he drifted back to being a loner. There was a hole in his life the size of Fremantle Harbour. He mucked around with Phillip and tried to help him along with the terrible bedwetting stuff, but you can't hang out with your ten-year-old brother *all* day.

He listened to the frogs in the swamp outside his window. Lockie figured one night this crummy old house would just sink into the slime – gloop, gloop, gloop – and in the morning there'd just be the wonky old TV aerial sticking up out of the mud. In a thousand years' time archaeologists would dig it up and find the Leonards – *homo swampus* – and they'd discover they'd been watching 'The Simpsons' all those years ago and eating cornchips. They'd find the ancient remains of lamb chops, peas and mashed potato on the table and they'd come across Lockie Leonard, human torpedo, lying on the ruins of his bed (still with the Sesame Street bedspread he had since he was four). His Mambo tee-shirt and Rusty boardshorts would identify him as a true grommet. Samples of his sunbleached blond hair would confirm this, as would the little bits of wax imbedded in the four hairs on his chest. And if anyone was in any doubt they only had to uncover the complete collection of Midnight Oil tapes under his bed and the *Surfing World* mags dating back to 1974.

In a thousand years, science would reveal that his tricky bits had taken a sharp blow from an obsolete Mark Richards quad-fin with a nasty ding on the left rail. Yes, under X-ray those goolies would have surfboard written all over them. But would scientists be able to tell that he was lonely? Fat chance. Would hot-shot gizmos show that his thirteen-year-old heart was broken by Vicki Streeton, that total spunk? Forget it. No way. No one now or in the future could know how rotten he felt inside.

Lockie closed his eyes and waited for the house to be swallowed up. Go on, let us have it! he thought. But you could tell by the chirpy sound of the frogs out there that nothing was going to happen tonight.

PULVERONIC ENGULFMENT

Next morning Lockie went back down the beach. Surfers are like that. They just never learn. Besides, Lockie figured being terrified was one way of taking your mind off things. Figure that out.

But when he climbed the last dune he knew that there was a limit to how much you really wanted to have your mind taken off things. The whole bay was off its face. On a scale from one to ten it was about 15¾. Even the fish were emigrating. The water surged up the dunes and smothered the islands. Each wave was like a building falling over. It was beyond nasty; it was one hundred per cent not-nice.

'You got a death-wish or something?' someone said behind him.

Lockie jumped. It was that pimply kid, Egg, complete with Pearl Jam tee-shirt and wraparound shades. He looked shocking.

'Some days,' said Lockie.

'But not today?'

'That's past death.'

'That's pulveronic engulfment.'

Lockie stared at him. 'What's that mean?'

'It's like decibelic heat-thrash.'

'What?'

'Voltageous chordage.'

'What language are you talking?'

'Me own, mate. Eggleston's Heavy Metal Dictionary, Part One.'

'You're joking.'

'Nope. I'm developing a new way of talking.'

Lockie stood there a moment. This kid with the Olympic pimples was in Year 9 *and* a bogan, and he was making his own language? A boofhead who was also a genius?

'You're not going in, then?' asked Egg, looking uncomfortably at the sea.

'No,' said Lockie. 'You?'

'Me? I can't even swim!'

Lockie scratched his blond mop. This kid was a phenomenon.

It was a bit of a walk back to Lockie's place, so Egg and Lockie talked to pass the time. They had weird things in common. They were city kids whose fathers got transferred here to the country. Without admitting it, they were both a bit bummed-out and lonely. Their dads had kooky jobs. Lockie and Egg both liked talking, too, and cracking dumb jokes.

Lockie started to like this kid, but he was dead nervous about being seen with him. I mean, the golden-haired surfrat walking along all matey with the black-shirted grunge-monkey. It was definitely bad for his reputation. Well, to hell with his rep, but it was still major culture clash. Lockie looked ahead and tried to see who was coming. He looked for familiar faces from school. He flinched when cars passed. Face it: Egg was a bogan and bogans were the *other* tribe; they were the enemy. Just why they were the enemy Lockie couldn't quite recall, but he was loyal to his surfing mates, even though he had none just now. Since Vickie Streeton dropped him like a hot spud, his friends had disappeared.

Lockie and Egg walked along in their different ways. Egg had that mean walk that bogans practise in the mirror. His black DB's were all over the footpath and his stick-on tattoos were starting to melt. Lockie swung along in his beachbum bounce that surfers polish up in their own mirrors, trying to look like an ad for muesli and Clearasil, but his one stubborn pimple gave him away. His ski-ramp thongs slapped and whumped up the hill. Together they were pretty funny to see, and of course everybody saw them, everyone knew. Angelus was a small town. Word gets out.

At the swamp, Lockie and Egg stopped to look at the shambles of a house the government had generously supplied the Leonard family. It looked like teachers had once lived in it.

'That's your place?'

'Yep.'

'Wow.'

'What would be your word for that?' asked Lockie.

'Floatatious.'

'One day it's gonna be a submarine. The TV aerial will be our periscope.'

'Wanna come to my place?'

Lockie shrugged. 'Orright.' He looked up and down the street. He stuffed his board deep into the reeds of the front yard and threw his towel in after it. Home was giving him the yips anyway.

HEAVY METAL

Egg's place was a bomb site. Lockie didn't know what to expect, but it sure wasn't this. The house looked fairly normal from the outside, but inside and out the back it looked like a terrorist attack. Everywhere you looked there was sheet-metal, steel, copper pipes, angle iron, aluminium tubing, rivets, tanks, car parts.

'As you can see my mum's into heavy metal as well,' said Egg sighing.

'Metal? This is junk.'

'Ssh! Are you nuts?'

'Ow!' winced Lockie. 'Don't even say that word!'

In the backyard, past the huge rusting racks that held steel sinks and baths, car bodies and parts, was a big open shed full of sparks. Someone was welding in there.

'That's my mum.'

'Welding?'

'Women weld too, you know.'

'I know that,' said Lockie, lying through his teeth.

'Come and have a look.'

They stepped into the shed where blue sparks sprayed across the floor and died at their bare feet. Mrs Eggleston threw back her helmet and looked at them. Her face was all red and sweaty.

'Mum, this is Lockie.'

'Hello,' said Lockie, looking at the hissing torch in her hand.

'How's your privates?' She was dead serious.

Lockie looked at Egg, dying. Aaagh!

Egg shrugged.

'Fine,' choked out Lockie. 'Thank you.'

'You wanna be careful,' said Mrs Eggleston.

'Yeah,' said Lockie. 'What're you building?'

'I don't build, I create,' she said and flipped her mask back down and went back to work.

Lockie leapt back from the sparks and the evil hiss of the flame and looked at Egg.

'She's a sculptor,' said Egg. 'Look.' He pointed at a pile of Holden wheelrims all welded together with hunks of steel bedframe. 'That's called "Autumn".'

Lockie stared at it. Next to it were two old baths stuck on top of each other. A little sign said, 'Bathmates'.

'Is she okay?'

'Some of the time.'

'Geez, I've got a horrible feeling the Sarge would like this stuff.' There, just behind, was the clutch plate of a '67 Cortina stuck on a shopping trolley full of housebricks.

'Is your dad a welder too?'

Lockie laughed. 'Sometimes he wishes he was.'

Lockie's dad saw himself as the last arty policeman. The Sarge said that if only people read poetry and washed their hands after going to the toilet, then the crime rate would fall away. He bored his prisoners into changing their ways.

Egg's room was the original Heavy Metal den. Across the door was a scrawl in felt pen: BON SCOTT LIVES! The walls were black and smeared with posters of Anthrax, Steve Vai, Megadeth, Iron Maiden, Judas Priest, and his bed was strewn with CDs and tapes of bands Lockie had never even heard of: Living Colour, Alice in Chains, Fishbone, Galactic Cowboys. In one corner on a silver stand stood a guitar, and beside his bed was an amplifier all kicked and scuffed and black. He wondered if Egg could play it. The room stank of socks and lost undies, underarms and zit cream. Kind of like his own, but more severe.

'Nice,' said Lockie, trying not to wrinkle his nose.

'Well, it's parent-proof. They hate it in here.'

'Too cheery for 'em,' said Lockie, looking at the posters full of black leather, studs, steel, and leering weirdos with guitars and hip boots. He pawed over the CDs sitting on Egg's swampy bed. All the songs were about war, suicide and the end of the world. Really optimistic – not!

'Heavy Metal,' said Lockie, shaking his head.

'I s'pose you like Madonna,' said Egg.

'Wash your mouth out,' said Lockie, deeply offended. 'I'm into Van Halen, actually,'

Egg laughed. 'That's Easy Listening, mate, mum-and-dad music. You're a real *surfer*.'

'Yeah,' said Lockie puffing up.

'It wasn't really meant as a compliment.'

'Oh.'

'I guess you like Midnight Oil, though. They're okay when they're a bit grungy.'

Lockie shrugged. 'I just think of Metal as boofhead music, you know? Panel-van noise.'

'Snob. Metal is a historical movement. You've heard of Jimi Hendrix, maybe? Deep Purple, Led Zep, Black Sabbath. It's the sound not the uniform.'

'But Anthrax? Megadeth?'

'Well, you've gotta start somewhere. I was nine. I'm into progressive Metal these days. You know,

24

King's X, Living Colour and some of that Seattle grunge.'

Lockie just stared. He had absolutely no idea what Egg was on about.

'Think of it as coffee. Van Halen is coffee with three spoons of sugar. This stuff is having it straight. The real thing.'

Egg slapped a tape into his deck and the most horrendous sound blasted out. It was like being sucked into the engines of a jumbo jet.

Someone appeared at the door. A little guy in a cardigan with an earring. He smiled briefly at Lockie and hammered on the doorframe but it was something you could only watch, not hear. This little bloke with the earring had a sort of slumped over defeated look about him, a sad look. In the end he went away.

'Who was that?' Lockie mouthed across the music.

'My dad,' mimed Egg.

Lockie's eyes widened. What a family.

Out of the window, propped up against the fence, Lockie saw a long, cigar-shaped piece of tin. Another sculpture, he guessed. But it had two holes in it. Lockie went over to the window and looked more closely. It was a kayak.

Egg turned the music off. 'What?'

'A kayak.'

'Yeah, Mum made it.'

'What's it called?'

'It's called a kayak that Mum made.'

'I've got an idea . . . '

'It's got a trailer, a bike trailer to tow it.'

'Does it float?'

'Never tried it. Mum was going through a phase, you know, trying to please me.'

'Did it work?'

Egg shook his head. 'Can't swim. Neither can Dad. And she's too busy with her own stuff. What am I s'posed to do with a two-hole kayak on me own?'

Lockie grabbed him by the arm. 'Let's go!'

LOSING YOUR FRUIT LOOPS

All the way through town, Egg towed that huge silver rocket of a thing on his trailer made of pram wheels and a bedframe while Lockie followed up behind, laughing all the way. People nearly drove off the road perving at them. It looked like two kids with an Exocet missile. Mrs Eggleston certainly built things to last. Egg's kayak was solid as a nuclear submarine. Going down hills, Lockie hoped Egg wouldn't have to brake suddenly. If that thing got going . . . He imagined it launching itself off the trailer, cutting Egg in half like a watermelon, and blasting into space.

Lockie thought about that so much he didn't notice Egg stopping in front of the town hall, slamming on the brakes to let some old lady make it over the crosswalk. He didn't even have time to brake. He ran up the back of the kayak, buried the wheels in the seat holes and left the bike altogether. Egg passed below him in a blur of pimples and Lockie collected the poor old lady on his way down. She broke his fall, you might say. Saved him a broken arm. He lay on the zebra crossing wondering if he'd killed an old age pensioner. Was he a granny slayer at thirteen? Imagine his joy when the old girl got up and started flogging into him with her handbag.

'Once a torpedo, always a torpedo!' someone familiar called.

Lockie looked around. Horns were parping at them now and the old lady was running out of puff on him. He knew that voice. His heart sank. There across the road in front of the town hall was Vicki Streeton. He wanted to dig into the asphalt and keep going till he got to Siberia but he had to get up, pull his buckled crate out of the kayak and clear the road.

They rode down to the harbour on the sheltered side of the peninsula where there were no waves and where the water wasn't quite so blue. Some kids fishing at the jetty saw them pass and Lockie

28

flinched a bit, hoping they didn't see him.

At the water's edge, Lockie sat in the kayak and pleaded.

'Come on, Egg, it's safe. See, no leaks. Your mum's an artist.'

'I just can't.'

'There's nothing to be nervous about. You can't fall out of this. See, you're tucked into a hole.'

'What if it rolls over?'

'This is the harbour, Egg. We're not going surfing on it. There's no rapids. Besides, you couldn't roll this thing without a winch anyway. This is a naval class craft. This is the original poo barge.'

'I've got this thing about sharks.'

Lockie clanged the side of the kayak. 'Mate. What sort of shark would try this on? This could be an icebreaker, a mine sweeper.'

'A coffin?'

'Geez, you're real cheery, Egg.'

'What about just in the shallow, then? For a start?'

Lockie sighed. 'Orright, jump in.'

'Just in the shallow.'

'Mate, if you fall out, I promise all that'll happen is you'll hit your head on the shore.'

Egg stood there a moment, his zits inflamed with worry, and then he finally sat down and took off his black ripple-soled desert boots.

That's when Lockie saw his toes for the first

time. On each foot there was something not quite right, there weren't enough toes. No, now that he looked – stared more like it – he saw that two toes of each foot were joined together.

'Hammer toes,' said Egg blushing till his zits went neon. 'I'm a Friday model.'

'Friday?'

'You know, like cars. A car built on a Friday is always junk. Everyone's always in a hurry to get it done and knock off for the weekend. I figure God was a bit distracted.'

Lockie looked at Egg and saw how miserable he was with himself. He really liked him.

'Get in.'

Egg got in with all the excitement of a sack of spuds, and Lockie pushed off. He passed a paddle forward to him and realized that Mrs Eggleston wasn't exactly a total genius. The paddles were made of steel. Arnold Schwarzenegger couldn't paddle with these things.

They got going somehow and Egg seemed to relax. The shallow end of the Harbour was dotted with half-sunk dinghies and riverboats with mountains of bird poop growing on them. Here and there was a submerged pram or a few tyres. On the surface, schools of plastic bags floated gracefully. It really stank. Angelus Harbour smelt like the boys' toilets in any school across the world.

Lockie steered them out into deeper water,

looking for something alive. There were no fish down there darting like sparrows way beneath them, that was for sure.

Then Egg got panicky and dropped his paddle. It sank like a brick and disappeared into the mud far below.

'Oops.' Oops? Flamin' oops?

Lockie spent the rest of the morning chauffeuring Egg around the harbour. His arms ached, but he enjoyed himself. Half the time they just floated about, lying with their heads on the warm tin casing of Mrs Eggleston's creation, finding out how different they were. Lockie liked yoghurt, summer, fluoro yellow, 'Northern Exposure', dolphins and *The Big Blue*. Egg was into choc-milk, winter, serious black, 'Roseanne', dung beetles and *This is Spinal Tap*. But they both hurled at the thought of Whacko Jacko, organized sport, advertising and Reeboks. It was a freaky meeting of minds.

'You still got the hots for Vicki Streeton?' murmured Egg as they drifted.

'Me? No. Yes. Well. I dunno. We had some fun. Didn't work out, you know.'

'You know I've never even had a girlfriend?'

'Really?'

'Fourteen, and I've never had a chick.'

'They don't like that, you know.'

'What?'

'Being chicks. And birds. And babes.'

31

'How come?'

'I dunno. Women. Who can understand 'em?'

'Yeah. Absolutely.'

Lockie smiled. He figured he could tell this kid anything. Egg was a thoughtful kind of guy, a smart bloke. This kid might end up being the best friend he ever had.

'I didn't expect your old man to have an earring.'

'Dad sees himself as a bit of a groover.'

'What's he like?'

'Oh, depressed.'

'I thought ministers were sort of . . . jolly all the time.'

'Oh, Dad has a hard time, I s'pose. Mum and him don't get on anymore. She doesn't wanna be a minister's wife. The church isn't too keen on him either. I reckon they're tryin' to get rid of him.'

'Cause of an earring?'

'No, he's just not what they had in mind.' Egg sighed and watched a mob of seagulls turning in the sky above them. 'And Mum and Dad just sort of hang together like two lumps of Play-doh. I think they're waiting for me to grow up and leave home so they can split.'

'What a bummer.'

'Yeah. I guess.'

Lockie felt the kayak brushing into a bank of reeds where the water was really foul.

'What about that music? Doesn't it make you feel worse?'

'No, not really. It kind of blasts you into numbness. It's more voidage than drasticality.'

'Voidage?'

'Blank, you know.'

'Oh.' Lockie thought about it. He was an optimist. He couldn't help it. Even at his worst Lockie still saw hope in things – he was that kind of kid. But he didn't have hammer toes and world series zits and parents who didn't like each other. Lockie didn't feel awkward just walking in public (unless it was with Egg). He was reasonably good looking and the only zit he had moved around his face like a nomad, camping for a day on his chin, moving overnight to the corner of his mouth to get out of the wind. Lockie had it easy compared to Egg. He was no genius, but he knew how lucky he was.

'What about . . . drasticality?'

Egg laughed. 'It means topping yourself, you know.'

'Suicide? Geez, Egg!'

'Calm down, son.'

'You don't think about that do you?'

Lockie sat up and looked at him. Egg lay there in front of him with his eyes closed against the blue sky. After a long time, Egg murmured. 'I have. Now and then.'

'Geez.' Lockie didn't know what else to say.

33

He lay back worried and thoughtful, looking at the sky, smelling the stinky water and hearing the reeds scrape by the tin canoe. A pouring sound, a kind of gurgling came from somewhere back in the reeds. It got louder all the time, and the water got smellier. Lockie eyes began to water.

'Whew,' said Egg. 'Was that you?'

'Get out of here,' said Lockie. 'Not even the Sarge could do that.'

The canoe began to snag in great slimy wads of algae. Lockie sat up and poled them through the green shallows where the reeds suddenly gave way to a paddock of floating grunge. It looked like a football team of giants had blown their noses into this corner of the harbour. Lockie began to feel queasy. He poled them right up beside a huge pipe that spewed into the waterway. On the algae-choked bank lay dead crabs and fish all snagged in weed so thick you could almost walk on it.

'Whew,' said Egg, 'what a nostril thrasher. This is sputagenous olfactorizing.'

'Eh?'

'It stinks to the max. On a scale of one-to-ten it's a – '

'Fifteen,' said Lockie. 'Who would do this? This is terrible.'

'Anyone who could get away with it.'

They looked at the steaming gunk that fell from the pipe and behind them the whole of Angelus

Harbour lay rancid and still, choking on algae and poison.

'Makes you sick, doesn't it?' said Egg.

But Lockie was too busy to answer. He was already losing his Fruit Loops and his five slices of toast and his morning cocoa over the side of the tin canoe. His ears rang. He saw blotches and stars and lights. He whooped up some nasty looking breakfast leftovers and he got mad as hell.

TAKING SIDES

After dinner that night Lockie still felt a bit crook, but not bad enough to get out of drying the dishes. He hated drying dishes because the Sarge always washed and the Sarge was a rotten washer-upper. Fast and useless, he got suds all over the kitchen and plenty of plates in the rack but everything was still covered in gloop that you had to wipe off yourself with the tea-towel.

'You still look a bit green,' said the Sarge from behind his Santa beard of bubbles.

'And I'm gunna do something about it, too,' said Lockie, wiping furiously.

36

'A lie down is probably best. I'll finish up here.'

'I mean about that stinking mess they're putting into the harbour.'

'It's pretty rotten,' said the Sarge.

'Rotten? It made me sick as a dog!'

'Well, you did paddle halfway up the pipe.'

'Sarge, I was on the harbour! Our town's harbour. People go swimming and fishing in that.'

'Mad sods.'

'It's right in the middle of the town!'

The Sarge wiped his sudsy beard off and looked at Lockie.

'But what can you do, mate?'

'I'm gunna stop it.'

'You're thirteen years old, Lockie.'

'How about you help me?'

The Sarge went back to washing up. 'I'm the Law, remember. I can't take sides. Besides we're still new here. I have to be a bit careful.'

'Sides? What about right and wrong?'

'Right and wrong aren't always the words I'm allowed to work with, mate. Try legal and illegal.'

Lockie chucked the towel on the sink and stamped off. Unbelievable! Of all people he figured the Sarge would be with him on this.

He slammed the door of his bedroom so hard the knobs fell off – plunk – inside – kerplunk – and outside. He lay on his bed fuming.

After a while his mum came knocking.

'Lockie?'

'Yeah.'

'Can I come in?'

'I guess. You pay the rent.'

'Where's the doorknob?'

'On the floor isn't it?'

'I can't see it anywhere. Just open up.'

'Orright.'

Lockie got up and found the doorknob on his side but when he tried to fit it back on it wouldn't go; it was bent out of shape.

'No good, Mum. I'm stuck.'

Lockie was half relieved. Mrs Leonard had come in for a heart-to-heart and she was a bit of a demon for parental talks, excruciating talks on any subject. It could be sex, homework, drugs, peer group pressure or screwing the lid back on the toothpaste. Whatever it was, it was always In-Depth. It was like being interviewed by '60 Minutes' on TV. Mrs Leonard called it 'Keeping in Touch'. Lockie called it major embarrassment.

There was a tap at the window and Lockie got up on one elbow to see his mum standing out in the dark, waiting patiently. You had to love her for it; she was like a dog at a bone.

Lockie pulled up the window.

'Nice try, love.'

'The knob *is* busted, honest.'

'Uh-huh.'

'Have a nice day, Mum?'

'Oh, I washed nappies, took Phillip to the park,

cleared the frogs out of the laundry. Pretty exciting. I didn't go swimming in industrial sludge, though, nothing exciting like that.'

'I wanna stop it, Mum.'

'So I gather.'

'I'm scared about the future.'

'The future usually looks after itself.'

'Are you with me or against me?'

'Well, I'm in the yard and you're in the house.'

'Can you help me?'

'Lockie I've got a baby and a lot of – '

'Orright,' said Lockie, flopping back onto his bed. 'Don't bother.'

'You don't have to speak to your mother like that,' said the Sarge suddenly appearing at the window.

'Sorry.'

Lockie's parents looked at each other and shrugged. Somewhere in the house Blob was trying to gnaw Phillip's leg off with her new tooth. It sounded like *The Texas Chainsaw Massacre*. Lockie stuck his fingers in his ears and closed his eyes. Aaarghhh!

ADULTS

Next morning Lockie went up to Egg's place. All the way up the street you could hear Nirvana screaming out of Egg's stereo. It sounded like a headbangers' thrash at the Baptist Church. It made Lockie smile. Definitely the church music of the future. Move over Mrs Pisslethwat and the plastic organ. Brethren, get down! Sisters, gimme high voltage! The minister playing guitar with his teeth. He could see it now.

In Egg's room the music was so loud you could almost see it like shuddering fog. Wallpaper started to peel. Egg's potted geranium looked punch drunk and deaf. Lockie felt nails rattling in the floorboards. It was a long time before Egg noticed Lockie. This was because Egg was on his back with his legs pedalling in the air. His attention was taken up with trying to be Angus Young from AC/DC. His guitar was an oversized wooden spoon, and he gave it all he had.

Lockie hit the stop button and Egg suddenly went scarlet.

'Oh. Hi.'

'Hi.'

'Just . . . doing my exercises.'

'It's orright,' said Lockie, trying not to smile. 'I use a tennis racquet. It's perfectly normal.'

Lockie and Egg wandered up to the local milk-bar without talking much. Lockie looked about carefully to check for passing surfers, but he was safe for the moment. Still, his feet sweated till his extra-wide thongs had puddles in them. Egg looked particularly boganic today. They shared a milkshake and then fed some change into a pinball machine that didn't stir. They stuck in some more money and didn't even raise a lightbulb. It just ate their money as if it was perfectly entitled to it. Lockie protested to the shopkeeper who threw them out and

41

told them never to come back. Lockie's rage returned.

'I talked to my oldies,' he said as they sat on the sticky pavement. 'People go brain-dead when they reach thirty.'

'My old man said he'd love to help us save the planet but he's too busy trying to save his job,' said Egg. 'Mum said we're all doomed anyway, so why bother.'

'See what I mean?'

Lockie kicked a Coke can across the pavement and the shopkeeper came and said he'd call the police.

'Call the police, then!' said Lockie.

'Oh, acquainted with the police, are you?' sneered the shopkeeper, a bald little bloke with a cascade of fat over his trouser belt.

'Daily,' said Lockie. 'You could say I'm in police custody every day of my life.'

The shopkeeper wrinkled his nose till it looked like a dried fig, then he slammed the door shut with a pretty tinkle of the bell.

'Adults,' said Lockie. 'Pathetic, isn't it?'

Lockie and Egg were halfway up the hill to the big empty school before the idea descended.

'John East,' said Lockie.

'What?'

'The Guidance Officer from school.'

'That hippy.'

'Exactly.'

'Exactly what?'

'I'm a genius. Let's go!'

THE LIVING
HAIR MACHINE

Lockie Leonard had a kind of love-hate rel-
ationship with the school Guidance Officer.
Not that he loved him – no fear, that was the
wrong choice of words, and he didn't really hate
him either. It was a sort of hot and cold business.
Sometimes Lockie thought John East was cool;
other times he saw him for what he was – an adult.
The bloke hung around school but wasn't a
teacher. He gave advice but didn't dish out work
or punishment. He was a mongrel breed, you could
say, but not a mongrel of a bloke. He talked to
you as if you were on his level. Trouble was, you

couldn't tell if his level was all that high.

John East lived up behind the pine forest in a sagging weatherboard joint where the grass grew as high as the windows. There was a tunnel from the letterbox to the front door, a sort of jungle track in the grass. Egg and Lockie clambered up onto the big wide verandah that looked out across the whole town and saw the junk lying around on it: a busted lawnmower, a garden gnome without a head, a stack of old newspapers, a surfboard. They looked at each other with raised eyebrows. A high-class lifestyle, no sweat. Lockie knocked on the flaky door.

After a minute or two, the door opened.

'Yeah?'

There he was in a pair of stripey pyjama bottoms in all his glory – the hairiest man on earth, half asleep.

'It's me,' said Lockie.

'Good,' said John East trying to pry his eyes open properly. 'Glad only one of us is confused.'

'Can we come in?'

John East looked at them and then past them to the day. 'What time is it?'

'Eleven,' said Egg. 'In the morning.'

'Damn – I was planning on sleeping in.'

'Sorry to wake you so early,' said Lockie with a smirk.

'You can watch me eat breakfast,' John East said, turning and heading back into the house.

Lockie and Egg just stared. The man had a back like a shag pile carpet. Every homeless hair in the universe had found its way to that back and taken root – black, grey, brown, white, long, short, straight, squiggly – it was a mohair masterpiece.

Lockie and Egg followed it down the hallway to the dingy kitchen that stank of damp socks and cigarette smoke. They sat down at the table and watched John East cook himself a spattering breakfast of bacon, eggs, tomato and baked beans. It was no hippy's breakfast. There were truck-drivers and mafia bosses who couldn't start a day with a meal like that. It was horrible to watch.

'You two are an unlikely pair,' he said gnashing away at his cholesterol feast. 'The headbanger and the surfrat. The original odd couple.'

'It's the future,' said Lockie shakily, half-believing it. 'I'm tomorrow and he's the day after.'

'Don't look at the uniform, that's our motto,' said Egg.

'Smart thinking, guys. What brought all this on?'

'Fate,' said Egg.

A simple whack in the goolies, thought Lockie grimly.

'What's the problem?'

'The harbour,' said Lockie. 'Last term you said something about the pollution in the harbour. Yesterday Egg and me went canoeing on it and got really crook. We wanna do something about

46

it. We thought you might help us, give us some ideas. Join us, maybe.'

'What are you calling yourselves – the Scumbusters?'

'Nice name for a band,' said Egg. 'Tomorrow and the Day After sounds cool, though.'

'Well,' said John East. 'I'm pretty busy . . . '

'Yeah, mowing the lawn and everything,' said Lockie with a grin.

John East scratched his chin. He had whiskers growing on his whiskers. The guy was a living hair machine. He got up and left the kitchen and when he came back he was dressed. He thumped a fat folder down on the table.

'It's all here.'

'What?' said Lockie.

'Two years ago the government did a study and gave the town and the industries around the harbour two years to clean up their act. Go home and read it.'

'All this?'

'Think of it as homework.'

'But this is the summer holidays!' cried Lockie.

'Good. Then you'll let me get back to bed?'

'We'll read it,' said Egg kicking Lockie under the table.

'You're a bit of a dark horse, Eggleston. A mystery man.'

'Everyone's a dark horse, sir.'

Lockie looked at Egg, dead impressed. Behind

that boofhead uniform was a smart person, someone worth knowing. He should quit being so damn embarrassed by him.

Egg gathered up the file and they headed for the door.

'It's your lucky week, boys.'

'How do you mean, sir?' asked Lockie.

'A friend of mine is coming down from the city to stay over Christmas.'

'Yeah. Great.'

'You ever heard of Queenie Coupar?'

They shook their heads, feeling dumb.

'This town used to be a whaling town, you know. Queenie helped that to change. You might find some expertise on hand, come the weekend. She's a real eco-guerilla.'

'A what?' said Lockie. 'A what gorilla?'

John East sighed. 'Do your homework, Lockie.'

Egg hauled him out the door and into the light of day.

'We're on our way,' said Egg.

'Where?'

Egg just shook his head and clutched the file to his chest. They fought their way through the jungle to the street.

BLAAH...

By five o'clock Lockie's eyes were like two raw meatballs and his butt was the shape of a pizza box. The kitchen table was piled with paper: graphs, cuttings, charts, reports, reports on reports, findings of reports on reports, letters about findings of reports on reports of reports. Aaargh! Egg lay his head on the table.

'How's it going there?' said Mrs Leonard.

'You ever heard of the death of a thousand cuts?' said Egg with a grin. All the blood had gone out of his face; even his zits were pale.

'Well, what does it mean?' Lockie's mum asked, slapping some lamb chops down onto the sink. Under the table, Blob gnawed at the lino, making disgusting dental noises.

'Yeah,' said Lockie. 'What does it all mean, Egg?'

'Don't you get it?'

'Mate, it's like Japanese algebra to me,' said Lockie, defeated.

Egg sighed. 'Well, the harbour's dying.'

'When things stink that bad they're usually dead, Egg.'

'It's dying because the seagrass is dying. Ninety per cent of the seagrass meadows that fish and stuff live and breed in are gone.'

'What killed them, Egg?' asked Mrs Leonard.

'Nitrogen and phosphates, mostly. From fertilizer. It makes algae grow. Algae stops the light getting through, the seagrass dies. The water goes bad.'

'Fertilizer? Is that all?'

'No, it's not the only problem. The harbour silt is full of heavy metals. Poison. The shellfish are poisonous, the fish are poisonous, those that are left.'

'That's terrible!'

'Now she listens,' said Lockie.

'Where's all this stuff coming from?'

'Lots of places. But mostly from the two factories that pump gunk straight into the harbour.

The fertilizer factory and the wool-mill.'

No one said anything for a few moments. Blob chomped away at the lino. Lockie rubbed his eyes. Egg scratched a zit. Mrs Leonard folded her arms, unfolded and then folded them again.

'And nothing's happening about it?'

'Not since this report came out. Two years ago. The factories had two years to clean up their act. Plus, the town itself was supposed to remove the algae and dredge the silt to get rid of the heavy metals.'

Mrs Leonard looked deeply thoughtful. 'Puts a new meaning on heavy metal doesn't it, Egg?'

Egg smiled. 'There's a difference, I guess.'

'Wanna stay for dinner?'

'Thanks, but I better go.'

Lockie climbed into his bed that night feeling depressed. His single pimple had moved to the end of his nose, as though it was bummed out, and ready to jump. He was healthy, he had a bed to sleep in and a room (that he had to share with a little brother, worst luck), and a family who loved him, but he still felt flat. No, worse, he felt a real dark sliding sadness in him. It wasn't like the miserable feeling he had after being dumped by Vicki Streeton. It was different, a weird creeping feeling. Lockie wondered if maybe this was what Egg felt like when he thought about drasticality. Such a smart kid. He wondered if depression was contagious. He couldn't even work up an Aaargh! All he felt was a kind of long, blue Blaaah.

HOT AS

Lockie paddled out into the glassy break and watched as some kid came howling across a long hollow wall of water at him, completely ripping up the wave. Right in front of him the other rider cranked a re-entry and floated in the lip above while he watched open-mouthed and too stunned to move. It was a she. A girl. One-piece speedos and pigtails. She came crashing down the face on the other side of Lockie who caught the full force of the wave and was ground mercilessly into the sandbar below.

He came up sputtering, cursing himself.

'You orright?' the girl said paddling by, her hair streaming water.

'Absolutely,' he honked, his nose full of water. 'No sweat.'

She just paddled by, her perky bum in the air and headed out again to the break. Lockie hauled himself sluggishly onto his board and followed, muttering.

It got worse. That girl spiked him for every wave that rolled in. She paddled like a demon and always got inside him. She took off right under the falling lip if need be. Late take-offs, freefalls, close outs, nothing bothered her. She was hot-as. It was pretty demoralizing. Not because she was a girl, but because he needed to blast away this miserable feeling that had been hanging on him for days now, and a surf was the only thing that could do it. And here he was, picking up scraps on his own break. And, yeah, maybe the fact that it was a girl just didn't help. Stupid, but true. What a caveman he was.

After half an hour Lockie just sat back and watched her. She was muscly and mobile and she had perfect wave judgement. She surfed like a total natural, for herself, as if no one else in the world existed. He had to admit it; she was even better than him and he was . . . well, excellent.

'You surf good,' he said as she paddled past, yet again.

'Thank you,' she said.

Then her smooth tanned face split in a smile. Her teeth were white and even her eyes were beautiful. It was a killer smile. It was like a bomb going off. He felt all busted up and confused inside. He wasn't ready for this. His heart was still hanging together with sticky-tape after Vicki Streeton and all along he knew that after Vicki anyone else would be second best. Lockie just sat there shuddering in the water like a stunned mullet. No. It wasn't possible. It wasn't right. That girl paddled off back to business and Lockie Leonard, for the second time in his life, felt himself dragged kicking and screaming into the twilight zone. Aaarrrrghhh! It couldn't be true. But it was. He was barking-mad, brain-dead leglessly in love.

LOVE'S VERY OWN
MICROWAVE

That night Lockie ran a bath so deep it was Jacques Cousteau material and the bathroom fogged up like a scene from a detective movie. Moisture ran down the walls. Rats and cockroaches gave up and moved back to the swamp. Lockie rubbed a clear spot in the mirror and looked at himself. Yes, that was the face of a man in trouble. His lonely single banger had moved up into his left nostril, probably in shame.

Lockie climbed into the barbarically hot water and tried to scrub the awful glow of love off himself. He used his mum's meanest floor-brush and a bottle of Vim and went at it till he looked like a prawn.

He didn't want any trouble.

Especially not when he'd just found a best mate, a truly best mate.

Besides, his poor, beat-up heart still had Vicki Streeton written all over it in fading red letters.

No, too complicated.

Bad timing.

Nope. Not again. No romance.

Please?

Lockie scrubbed and rubbed. He poked and soaked. He held his breath and lay under the scalding water, refusing to let himself up till he got a grip and changed his ways. But it was no use. He came up gasping and still the sinking torpedo he was.

He stayed so long in the bathroom his parents started to get suspicious and the Sarge called out that he might go blind. There was a lot of laughing out there. He concentrated on shaking this business off. But when he climbed out of that great stewing tub to look at himself in the mirror again, he saw that he was a complete goner.

Towelling himself off, he thought of that smile, that perky set of speedos, that head of hair, that . . . that girl. Hell, Vicki dumped him, didn't she? She was no lump of perfection. Dropped him before an audience of millions, in front of the whole world. And there at the beach today was this hot grommet smiling at him till he thought his very buns would burst. So where was the problem?

Lockie Leonard came out of that bathroom glowing and steaming like he'd just stepped out of love's very own microwave.

HAS A CHICKEN
GOT LIPS?

Egg and Lockie decided they had to start somewhere, so they wrote up some handbills for a letter drop and Egg photocopied a thousand of them and blew up his dad's Xerox machine. Actually, it belonged to the church and didn't help things for Rev Eggleston that week.

SAVE OUR HARBOUR!
Angelus Harbour, one of the most
excellent natural harbours in
Australia, is poisoned and polluted.
Two years ago the EPA demanded a

clean-up but NOTHING HAS BEEN DONE.
Mussels, crabs, and fish are
poisonous! Our harbour is dangerous!
Our town stinks! Public meeting at
7.30pm, 22 December, 5 Drain Street.
Be there or be a mutant!

Egg hauled them to Lockie's on his kayak trailer, his ears still ringing. Funny how parents could hurt your ears. Heavy metal never did that.

Lockie lay on his bed with an expression that reminded Egg of a garden gnome.

'What's up with you?'

'Hm?'

'Lockie? Are you conscious? Are you alive?'

Lockie nodded vaguely. A person in love is a sad sight. They give garden gnomes a bad name.

'I've got the handbills.'

'Great.'

'Great? I nearly got kicked out of house and home! What's the matter with you?'

Lockie just lay on his bed looking at the ceiling. It was disgusting to watch.

'Are you taking diet pills or something?'

Lockie blinked.

Egg grabbed him by the ears and shook him till his brain rattled like dice in a cup.

'Earth to Lockie!'

'Sorry. What were you saying?'

Mrs Leonard came in and stood at the doorway.

'I've seen him like this before. He's met a girl.'
'How depressing,' said Egg.
'Hm?' said Lockie.
'Tomorrow is on pause, I think.'

Out on the streets of Angelus they weaved and wobbled on their bikes, stuffing letterboxes with their handbills. They were chased by dogs and shouted at by suspicious old people, almost flattened by trucks. The awful glow faded on him as the day went on, but his mind was never really on the job. In the main street he put his front wheel down a storm grate and lost two hundred handbills in one white cloudburst that he chased around the streets for half an hour. He copped endless lip from Wacker Newman and Rudi Dudah from his English class. Word was out on him and Egg. Lockie was a traitor, they said. He ignored them best he could, but it hurt getting ragged by second-rate surfers.

Mrs Leonard pushed Blob around the neighbourhood in the pram and Phillip helped her give out four hundred until he got his hand caught in the spring-loaded mouth of a letterbox which the Fire Brigade had to saw open with the Jaws of Life.

At John East's house Lockie and Egg hacked their way through the rolling savannah grasslands, the vast romantic prairie of his front yard to bang on the door and give him fifty or so to hand out to teachers and neighbours. But for all their knocking they couldn't raise him so they left them there and did the full Burke and Wills back to the street.

Lockie gave a handbill to the grumpy owner of the milkbar who called him a communist and a trouble maker and several things that made his hair stand on end but he enjoyed the experience anyway.

At the end of the day everybody was sore and fed up but glad to have got the job done. Egg went home to face the music from his dad, and Lockie soaked his saddlesore bum in another hot bath.

Mrs Leonard came in and Lockie grabbed a flannel and camouflaged himself.

'Getting shy are we?' she said with a grin.

'No, I was just reaching for the flannel and dropped it as – '

'Calm down, it's normal enough. You're in the bathroom a lot, these days. You're going through puberty, Lockie.'

'Mum – '

'Every boy and girl – '

'Mum – '

'Begins to feel their body change – '

'Mum!'

Lockie wished he could duck dive down the plughole. Couldn't she leave puberty alone for five minutes?

'He'd rather not talk about puberty right now, Mum,' said Phillip, coming in behind her to show off his flash bandage. 'Anyway, what's puberty?'

'Phillip!' Lockie wailed. 'Don't start her off again!'

'Lockie's embarrassed by his changing body.'

'Looks the same to me,' said Phillip.

'Phillip, go and check on Blob. She's probably eating something.'

'Yeah, the sofa maybe,' Phillip said heading out.

Lockie lay back in the bath. 'Anyway, thanks for helping, Mum. It was great.'

'No problem,' she murmured. 'I just hope we can cope with all the people tomorrow night. Your father's going to have a fit.'

'Haven't you told him?'

'Well, put it this way: he's not in possession of all the facts.'

'Funny, you know. I thought he'd be right behind us.'

'He's in a really awkward position, Lockie. Try to understand. Anyway, what are you going to say to this crowd tomorrow night?'

'Egg said we should wait for inspiration. His dad's a minister, you know.'

'That's what I'd call flying by the seat of your pants.'

'Don't remind me. The seat of my pants has got blisters.'

'Want me to take a look?'

'Mum, has a chicken got lips?'

MUSICAL CHAIRS

All Friday afternoon Lockie and Egg paced, waiting for inspiration, but all they got was perspiration and sore feet. They carried chairs two at a time from the church hall down the hill to Lockie's place until Egg's dad hit the roof and went into a mental meltdown. They arranged the loungeroom at Lockie's so that forty people could squeeze in and have their feet gnawed and slobbered on by Blob.

Phillip and Mrs Leonard made chocolate crackles and lamingtons and the kitchen slowly turned brown.

The only meeting Lockie had ever spoken at was the night he'd been thrown out of the Angelus Surfriders' Club of which he was the president. It wasn't much of a speech and it wasn't much of a club and it was a shambles of a meeting. Lockie started to shake at four o'clock in the afternoon.

'Calm down,' said Egg. 'It's just a group of people.'

'What if we get hecklers?'

'Hecklers, jecklers, who cares?'

'Why don't you do the talking? You're older.'

'More people know you,' said Egg. 'You went out with Vicki Streeton once, remember.'

'I don't wanna put me dad in an awkward position.'

'Fair go, Lockie! I almost got my old man the sack! I even knocked off the church urn for all the cups of tea!'

Egg had him there. It was down to Lockie.

By six o'clock he could hear his heart beating in his ears. It sounded like Phil Collins on steroids.

At six-thirty he got a dose of Kalahari mouth. He couldn't get up enough spit to swallow water.

Six forty-five he got a bad case of the trots and wouldn't come out of the toilet till seven-fifteen.

At seven-fifteen Phillip got the trots but it was probably all the cocoa from the chocolate crackles he'd eaten, so Lockie was hooked out and replaced.

By seven-thirty they were reeling and quaking at the front door. Egg's face glowed. Lockie's teeth chattered.

They were still there at eight. And at eight-thirty.

At nine they turned the urn off. At nine-thirty they silently stacked the chairs and the Sarge came home off his shift.

'Ah, musical chairs,' he said. 'My favourite!'

X Marks the Dot

Half the morning Lockie lay in bed feeling out-
raged, ashamed and depressed, until Egg
came round and hooked him out.

'C'mon, get dressed.'

'I am dressed. Where are you going?'

'*We* are going to have it out with someone.'

'John East.'

'You're a genius, Leonard. Geez, brush your
teeth, willya? You smell like you been gargling
the harbour.'

As they headed for the door, Mrs Leonard
called: 'Aren't you going to have something to

eat? You can't start the day on an empty stomach, you know – ' But they were gone before she got a reply.

As he rode alongside Egg, Lockie looked at the houses of the town. Today they all looked closed-up and sleepy. People's cars looked stupid and shiny, their lawns suddenly ridiculous in their smoothness.

'I hate this town.'

'It's just a normal town,' said Egg.

'I can't believe no one came.'

'Bit of a disaster, eh.'

'We gotta do something.'

'We keep saying that, Lockie. Who's gonna listen to two kids?'

Lockie gritted his teeth. He never felt so mad.

At John East's house they nearly beat the door down. Lockie was sweaty and revved up by now; he was ready to go for the throat. When the door finally opened, his mouth was already in fifth gear.

'So where were you then, eh? Where did you . . . '

Lockie's voice trailed off as he saw who it was opening the door. She wore a Hot Tuna tee-shirt with the sleeves cut out and a pair of boardshorts. Her hair was half wet and Lockie could smell shampoo and conditioner. Her brown skin shone like wood. Her eyes were blue and she looked ready to punch someone's head in.

'You? You!' said Lockie with his jaw sinking so low he had to slouch to make words.

The girl looked at him as if he'd just had his legs waxed and his head sawn off. His heart went into a meltdown; he heard sirens and horns, and red flashing lights went off in front of his eyes.

'Do I know you?' she said, looking doubtfully at him.

'The beach,' said Lockie. 'The other day.'

She shrugged. 'John! There's a couple of . . . blokes here to see you, I think.'

Egg looked at Lockie and tried to wake him up a bit, but Lockie was glowing like a nuclear beetroot.

'You don't remember, then?' said Lockie.

The girl looked at him again, up and down. Wrinkled shorts and shirt, chewed old thongs, his hair wild and greasy. 'Oh, yeah. You got pounded. I remember. Here's John.'

John East came to the door with a mug of coffee in his hand.

'Ah, it's Tomorrow and the Day After.'

'We're more interested in last night,' said Egg, 'You didn't come.'

'As you can see, my friends arrived.'

'You didn't come,' said Lockie watching the girl walk back down the hall to the kitchen.

'How did your meeting go, anyway?'

'No one came,' said Lockie.

'But thanks for asking,' said Egg, turning to go.

'Stay for a cuppa.'

'I don't think so,' said Egg, stepping off the verandah.

'A cuppa'd be great,' said Lockie.

'What?' said Egg in disbelief.

'I could really go a cuppa,' said Lockie.

'Right, then, I'll put the kettle back on.'

Egg scowled at Lockie all the way down the hall. Lockie had that garden gnome look back in his face. It was not a dignified sight.

The kitchen was a mess of dishes and news-papers and bits of bread crust and at the table sat a man and a woman. The bloke was thin and going a bit grey; he had a friendly enough face and looked like he'd just crawled out of bed. The woman was like a grown-up version of surfer-girl: honey-coloured hair, smooth skin, a bit mus-cular and very pretty.

'Boys, this is Cleve and this is Queenie. And I gather you've already met Dot,' said John East casually. 'And these specimens are two reprobates from my school.'

Dot? What kind of a name was *that*? And what was all this *reprobates* bollocks?

'Lockie here, and Egg.'

'Otherwise known as Tomorrow and the Day After.'

'Well, we're the future,' said Lockie.

'A bit of it, anyway,' said Egg, kicking him in the leg.

'Hi, fellas,' said Cleve.

'G'day,' said Queenie.

Dot said nothing. She stood by the sink with a piece of toast and Lockie stared hopelessly at her, all the fight and fury gone out of him. Egg elbowed him, trying to stir him into speaking, but Lockie had forgotten his speech.

'We wondered why you didn't come to the meeting?' said Egg. 'We sorta thought you'd be there, you know.'

John East sat down and got stuck into a plate of eggs and bacon. Man, he loved that cholesterol.

'Oh,' he said with his mouth full, 'I had to go out and help these guys.'

Cleve groaned. 'I did a fan belt about thirty k's out of town. What a performance.'

'Oh,' said Egg.

'Oh,' said Lockie, watching Dot's beautiful cheeks going in and out on a helpless bit of toast.

'What sort of meeting did you have?'

Egg rammed Lockie harder this time. 'What sorta meeting did we have, Lockie?'

'The sort that no one comes to,' said Lockie miserably.

'I think I've discovered a couple of real eco-guerillas here,' John East said to Queenie. 'You might be able to give them a few tips.'

71

Queenie rolled her eyes. 'My protesting days are over, mate.'

'We heard you closed down the whaling,' said Lockie politely.

'Well, I tried.'

'It worked didn't it? Eleven years later, there's whales out there and no whalers.'

'True. I guess.' She smiled. Lockie liked her straight out, and not because she was the mother of the hot grommet by the sink, but because she seemed kind of open-hearted or something. Strong, straightforward, free of bulldust. He decided all this in twelve seconds which was a long time by Lockie's standards.

'What are you having meetings about?'

'The harbour.'

'Aha. So it's finally happened. Someone's woken up.'

'It's really desperate,' said Egg. 'No one's doing anything, not even the things the law says they have to do.'

'Sounds normal for around here.'

'I just don't get it,' said Lockie. 'Why are they letting it get so bad?'

Queenie sighed and put down her cup of tea. She looked out the window a few moments and said,

'How long have you got?'

'All day,' said Egg.

'I'm going for a surf,' said Dot. 'Is that okay?'

Cleve nodded. 'Be careful. I'll pick you up in two hours.'

'I might have to go somewhere too,' said Lockie. 'Remember that . . . that thing, Egg?'

'No,' said Egg through his teeth. 'I don't.'

'Oh. Okay. Fine.' Inside he was going Aaarghh! out of sheer frustration and love. He ached. He was completely blitzed. He hardly heard a word that was said. On and on it went in that bombshelter kitchen of John East's, and all he could think of was Dot. Dot. What a romantic name, he thought. Dot. It had poetry in it. X marks the Dot. Dot! In the name of love! Mate, he was a goner.

PAINT ME GREEN
AND CALL ME GUMBY

When they beat their way back to the road through John East's Kakadu of a front yard Egg was furious with Lockie. His face glowed so red it looked like he might go up in flames.

'What the hell is it with you?' he hissed. 'You were a moron in there, a complete dickhead! We're talking about really important stuff with people who can really tell us things, help us out, and you come on like it's got nothing to do with you, like the harbour's not something on your mind. Mate, I was totally, totally embarrassed. I was ashamed to the max. You even made me look like a bumscrape, and I don't deserve it.'

Lockie shrugged. 'I'm going down the beach. Wanna come?'

Egg looked at him in disbelief. 'No, I don't.'

'Orright. See ya.'

'What, is it Ken and Barbie now? Surfer girl and surfer boy, a beautiful meeting of hormones. I thought we were mates.'

'We are,' said Lockie. 'I'm only going to the beach, Egg.'

'Well, you let me know when you land back on planet earth!' said Egg, who turned and walked away down the hill, kicking a can all the way down the street with his beetle crushers.

Man, what's wrong with him? thought Lockie, heading off toward the beach.

Lockie sat on the top of a dune and watched the figure alone out there on the flat sea. Not a wave in sight. The ocean looked washed and ironed; it was a pretty depressing sight. It was warm there without any wind and Lockie took off his shirt. He got comfortable and bunched his shirt up behind his head and lay there still watching. There she was, just sitting in the flat sea, just sitting.

He woke with a start. Water. Water was dripping on him. He looked up and saw Dot Cookson in her wetsuit, her board under her arm, looking down at him.

'I see you're working flat out for your country,' she said without a smile.

'Uh? Oh, yeah,' he stammered, sitting up. 'I was just – '

'Spying on me?'

'No, just watching.'

'What's the diff?'

'I dunno,' admitted Lockie.

Dot turned aside and cleared her nose – a classic bushman's blow – as he looked on in horror. Geez, that was hardly poetry in motion. He did it himself after a surf – had to – but he was a bloke, wasn't he?

'Charming,' he said, feeling for his wandering pimple.

'Where's your mate?'

'Egg? He went home.'

'Egg? What kind of a name is that?' she said, squeezing water from her hair.

'Like Dot, I s'pose. Economical, huh?'

She smiled and Lockie's heart started doing the bloodbank tango. His teeth chattered, his toenails started to curl up. Yikes! It was safer when she frowned.

'H – h – how long are you down for?'

'I dunno. Till after Christmas. It's a boring little town, eh?'

'I used to think that,' said Lockie. 'I only moved

here at the beginning of this year. But I really like it now.'

'Surf's mostly rotten.'

'You shoulda been here last week.'

'Everyone says that.'

Lockie laughed. 'But this time it's true. What school do you go to?'

'North Beach.'

'I didn't know they had a high school.'

'Oh, it's not a high school.'

Lockie grabbed two handfuls of sand in shock. Wait a second. Hang on here.

'Not a high school?' he squeaked feebly.

'North Beach Primary,' she said with a killing grin.

Lockie felt the dune turning to quicksand. He was history. He was in love with a girl in primary school and his life wasn't worth living!

'How . . . how . . . um . . . how old are you, then?' It was all a mistake! This kid was fourteen if she was a day. Lockie Leonard knew what humans looked like at fourteen, didn't he?

'Eleven,' said Dot. 'I'm twelve later this month.'

Lockie couldn't even say the word, so he mouthed: E-L-E-V-E-N-?

Aaarghhh!

They looked at each other a few moments.

'Well,' said Lockie. 'Paint me green and call me Gumby.'

'What?'

'I thought you were fourteen.'

Dot laughed. She seemed positively delighted and that made him even more depressed.

'I go to high school next year.'

'Great,' said Lockie glumly.

'How old are you?'

'Thirteen,' he answered.

'Unlucky number.'

'You better believe it,' said Lockie with conviction. 'There's a big difference between twelve and fourteen.'

'You walking back?'

'Yeah,' said Lockie. 'Me car's in for a tune up. Bit of a hassle.'

She laughed sweetly and Lockie's heart went from tango to funeral march. Dot Cookson. Eleven and three quarters and beautiful as Elle MacPherson and here he was, horribly, drastically, hideously in love. He felt guilty about Vicki, embarrassed about Dot's age, angry at himself for being such a pushover for romance. He was desperately mixed up.

Lockie turned his head politely as Dot pulled off her wetsuit and dried off her speedos with a towel. Well, he peeked. Perved, really. She had a body like an Olympic swimmer, like a triathlete; she made him look like a sausage skin full of lumpy custard. Man, she had arms like a truckdriver.

Dot pulled on a pair of shorts and ripped off

another bushman's blow that sent snot and seawater all over the dune.

'You're . . . you are good at that,' he said, as they set off.

'Practice makes perfect.'

'I went into a newsagent's once after a surf. Me nose all plugged up with water, you know. Anyway, I'm leaning over having a perv at a *Tracks* mag when – whoosh – out comes fifty litres of snot and ocean all over the magazine rack. I had to buy the surf mag and two *Women's Weekly*s. The guy chucked a mental.'

'Well, blow before you go.'

She's really romantic, thought Lockie. Here we are talking about sinuses!

They walked up toward John East's place talking about dumb stuff or not talking at all. As they went Dot smiled more and more, and curious kids rode by trying to suss out who Lockie Leonard was with, some girl carrying his surfboard. Man, did he have them eating out of his hand, they thought.

'Well,' he murmured at the top of the hill, 'I go down there.'

'The swamp?'

'Yeah, the swamp.'

'Well, I'm going back to the jungle,' she said with a laugh that put his heart back into fast forward. 'John's lawn hasn't been cut for a hundred years.'

'How come you guys know him?' Lockie asked.

'Oh, ancient history. Whales, I guess. He reckons you're a smart kid.'

Lockie's jaw dropped. 'Me?'

'Yeah, he reckons you're okay.'

Lockie was dumbfounded. And flattered. Well, sort of. If an old person liked you, it could mean there was something daggy about you; it wasn't always a good sign.

'Might see you down the beach tomorrow,' said Lockie.

'Yeah, maybe.'

'Well.'

'Yeah.'

'Seeya, then,' said Lockie.

'Yeah, seeya,' said Dot, not moving. A big gorgeous smile came to her face.

'What?'

'Maybe he's right,' she murmured. 'Maybe you are okay.'

Lockie's knees did a drum solo. Bushman's blow or no bushman's blow, this girl was fabulous. 'Oh, he's right, alright. There's nothing wrong with me that a few brains and million bucks wouldn't fix.'

He turned and bolted down the hill. He just couldn't hang around any longer – it was killing him. He was a cradle snatcher. He had the hots for a kid in *primary school!* Hell, he should be locked up. He was a living disgrace. It wasn't fair.

80

CHRISTMAS EVE

Lockie waited all morning for Egg to come over but he never came. It was Christmas Eve and they were supposed to go shopping together today. Everyone at home was pretty chilly on him, now that he noticed. His mum kept her distance, and Phillip who'd had a relapse of bedwetting wouldn't come near him either. Lockie's pimple went a real Christmassy red and moved toward his chin.

He broke open the biscuit tin that contained all his savings. Nineteen bucks. He hunted down the back of the lounge chairs and in the linty cleavage of the old Falcon's upholstery to scrounge up another eighty-six cents. $19.86, that was it. Grand total.

'That's not your money,' Phillip said darkly. 'The change in the seats is everyone's.'

'Finders keepers,' said Lockie. 'Anyway, what's wrong with you lot?'

'Ask yourself,' said Phillip going inside.

'Mum?' Lockie called. 'I'm going to Egg's and we're going Christmas shopping!'

Mrs Leonard at the clothesline just shrugged. He went off shaking his head.

Egg wouldn't come to the window. Lockie knew he was there; he banged away on the glass until putty started to fall out of the panes, but the curtain didn't move.

'What's up with *you*?' he called at his own reflection in the glass. 'I thought we were going Christmas shopping!'

Suddenly, the tapedeck blasted into life – AC/DC at full volume – and Lockie reeled back into the picket fence. Geez, it was like a brick in the face, that music. Well, let him be like that. He'd go on his own.

The little town was full of shoppers and people trying to park Fairlanes and Landcruisers up and down the main street. The stink from the harbour was humungous – truly unpleasant, but Lockie had his mind on other things.

The first major Christmas present he saw was a tee-shirt hanging in the window of Bert's House of High Fashion. Bert's was the kind of shop that sold clothes and novelties. You know, things like rubber sick and onion-flavoured chewing gum. It made K-Mart look severely up-market. The tee-shirt had printed on the front:

FASHION CAPITALS OF THE WORLD
NEW YORK
PARIS
ROME
ANGELUS

Lockie coughed up fifteen bucks and had it gift-wrapped for Dot. That left him $4.86 to spend on his family. Which was a bit of a problem. $4.86 between four people.

That morning, Lockie ducked in and out of every shop in Angelus. He tried the secondhand store, the St Vincent de Paul; he looked for freebies at the Tourist Bureau and scoured the racks of every newsagent for a comic the whole family might enjoy, but in the end he went to Woolworths and bought $4.86 worth of chocolate caramels.

He was walking home when the police car pulled over by the kerb in front of him. The Sarge wound down the window.

'Doin' the old Chrissie shopping, eh?'

'Yep,' said Lockie, looking around to see if anyone he knew was watching.

'Just let me know if you need the trailer to bring it all home in.'

'I will.'

'Jump in, I'll drive you home.'

Lockie got in and sank down in the seat.

'You okay?' asked the Sarge.

'Yeah.'

'You've been a bit funny lately.'

'Funny?'

'Odd. Peculiar. Out of sorts. Strange. You want more?'

'No.'

'Are you having growing pains?'

'Sarge – '

'You know about the onset of puberty, I imagine – '

'Dad – '

'Pubic hair . . . your voice begins to change . . . '

'Sarge!'

'You know about drugs?'

'Oh, please!'

'Is it your goolies still? Testicles are very delicate . . . well, things.'

'Sarge, I'll jump out of the car.'

The Sarge shrugged and drove home the rest

of the way in silence, looking sideways every now and then at the presents in Lockie's lap. Lockie just thought about Dot Cookson.

That night the Leonards went up the hill to the Baptist Church for Carols By Candlelight. Everyone sang their hearts out and burnt the hair off their arms and got hot wax all over themselves, but it sounded like angels all over the neighbourhood.

Egg's dad led the singing with a big toothy smile, but he looked sick to Lockie. Mrs Eggleston sang grimly through her teeth. Egg sat way over to the side in a thick cloud of midges and didn't sing at all. Lockie tried to catch his eye but got nowhere. His parents sang so loud he expected birds to fall from the sky.

Hark the herald angels sing!

Lockie thought of Dot.

Silent night, hoooooly night!

Dot Cookson.

We three Kings of Orient Arrre!

Dot.

While sheperds watched their flocks by night all seated on the . . .

Dot.

Dot.

Dot.

Dot.

He left without seeing Egg. He went home and looked at the Christmas tree in the loungeroom and heard the Sarge's Perry Como Christmas record and let everyone kiss him goodnight, but he was thinking of her all the time.

In his bed with Phillip chatting to him in the warm dark, it was like a woodpecker in his brain:

Dot – dot – dot – dot – dot . . .

STENCH

On Christmas Day the town stank. We're talking putrid, here. Through every open window came the smell of a lifetime. People blamed their dog or the bean tacos of the night before. They called the plumber who was off for Christmas; they emptied fridges and looked under the shrubbery for dead cats. Christmas trees wilted, even the plastic ones, and people's appetites took a bit of a hiding. There were roasts and puddings half eaten all over Angelus, that day.

No one checked the fridge or looked for dead cats at the Leonards' place, though. They knew what it was: the harbour.

'I think you and Egg better get to work on this,' said Mrs Leonard over her half-eaten meal. 'Lockie? You listening?'

'Huh?'

'The harbour. What're you going to do?'

'The adults made the mess,' he murmured, 'let them figure it out.'

Lockie's mum just looked at him in disbelief.

'Hey, Lockie,' said Phillip, 'Thanks for the caramels. You left the price on. $4.86. You really went crazy over us.'

'Phillip,' said Mrs Leonard.

'Gratitude,' said Lockie.

'Well, there's one present still under the tree,' said Phillip.

'That's private,' said Lockie. 'I'll deliver it later.'

'To whom?'

'Whom? What are you Phillip?'

'Lockie!' snapped Mrs Leonard.

'Merry Christmas, everybody!' said Lockie, kicking back his chair and heading for his room.

Just then, the Sarge came in from the split shift and threw his cap and handcuffs on the table.

'Whew! It's nasty out there. Happy Christmas everybody!'

Everybody stood glumly where they were before he came in.

'What's this? I work all Christmas morning in a town that stinks like the end of the world, and

I get home to a house full of statues. Is this the twilight zone, or what?'

Lockie mumbled season's greetings and went to his room. He put on his new Mambo shirt and his Billabong boardshorts, scrubbed his teeth with a finger and looked at himself in the mirror. Hmm. Not bad.

Lockie beat his way up the hill toward John East's place. All over Angelus, kids were hacking around on new bikes, fighting over cricket sets and computer games and snagging their shiny kites in power lines. He clutched Dot's Christmas gift under his arm and rehearsed a few slick lines. He had to be careful; he'd never been the older man before.

Now and then a gust of wind would get up and bombard the town with that harbour stench and the grass would lie flat and birds stagger in mid-flight. Lockie paid no attention. He worked on his opening sentence and broke into a nervous sweat.

By the time he hacked his way through the national park of John East's front yard, the gift wrap around Dot's tee-shirt was starting to come away in little bits like spitballs. Every time Lockie tried to push it all back together, bits stuck to his fingers and made it worse. It looked like it had been savaged by a dingo.

He banged on the door and waited. And waited. It was the middle of the afternoon and there wasn't a sound.

'Anyone home?' he shouted through the keyhole.'Ho! Ho! Ho! It's Santa here!'

But not a peep.

Miserably, Lockie left the pulpy parcel on the step and slunk off.

But there was no eerie silence at Egg's place. All hell was breaking loose when Lockie walked down the driveway.

'Alright then, let them do it, the mental pygmies!' screeched Mrs Eggleston.

'Don't start, woman! Just don't start!' bellowed Mr Eggleston.

There were pots and walls crashing; you could hear it from the street. They were shouting and ranting and crying in there and it was truly awful to hear.

'I hate this stinking town anyway! Can't you smell it? It's corruption, greed, stupidity – '

'Shut up, for pity's sake!'

'And you're too weak to stand up against it!'

Lockie stood hesitantly in the drive a few moments. Poor Egg. Christmas Day and your oldies chucking a mental. Maybe I better see if he's alright.

He found Egg out in the big shed full of steel

sculptures and welding gear. He was hunched up by the oxy cylinders bawling and sniffing and kicking the concrete floor.

'Egg?'

Egg looked up and wiped his face.

'Piss off, Lockie.'

'Mate, I just – '

'You deaf? I said piss off!'

Lockie stood there, completely miserable. 'Come over to my place for a while, eh?'

'What, isn't your girlfriend home?'

Aargh! That stung. Because it was true. Here he was, at his best mate's place because Dot wasn't in. Guilty. Man, what a creep he was.

'Carn, let's go for a walk, Egg.'

'Leave me alone.'

'Egg, mate – '

Suddenly Egg grabbed a lump of iron pipe from the floor and held it like a baseball bat.

'You've got three seconds! You hear me?'

Lockie went. He was nearly bawling himself. Man, what a mess. His whole life was a wipeout.

VISITORS

Lockie stopped in his own driveway and looked at the strange Land Rover parked out the front of his house. His heart sank even further – it was dragging somewhere down inside his pelvis now – and he tried to think if he had any relatives with a Land Rover. Who else would visit on Christmas Day? Rellies. Aaargh. Death by boredom.

The cop car peeled away from the house, out from behind the battered 4x4, and came walloping down the bumpy drive. The Sarge pulled up beside Lockie.

'Reckon you'd better get in there, mate. The house is full of subversives.'

Lockie blinked. 'Rellies?'

The Sarge laughed and hit the blue light just for the hell of it.

'No, your teacher mate and his friends.'

Lockie gulped. 'Oh.' Oh? Oh – oh!

'Hey, by the way, is that her?'

'Her?'

'The cause of all this achey-breaky heart stuff. You know, daydreaming with little fat hearts coming out of your ears all day.'

'Dot?'

'One syllable and look at him,' the Sarge chuckled. 'I s'pose that's her, then. What else could turn my eldest son into a walking beetroot? Well, you better get into your shining armour, Sir Lockie. I've got crime to fight. I'll leave love to you.'

Laughing madly, the Sarge planted his foot and fishtailed up the drive in a blast of dirt. Sometimes Lockie thought his father should be locked up.

Full of dread, he trudged up toward the house. Man what a Christmas.

He stopped at the front door and decided it would be smarter to sneak in the back way, so he went into a commando crouch through the weeds and under the clothesline, going so fast he didn't recognize that pair of brown feet until too late. He hit Dot like a half-back and she went down with a great oof of a thud.

For a moment he just lay there stunned with the point of his chin in her belly button until she whupped him on the head with her knuckles.

'Get off me, you boofhead!'

'Um – '

'Get off!'

She swatted and cracked him till he got up and offered her his hand which she refused indignantly. She got up on her own.

'You orright, Dot?'

'What are you doing?'

'Going in the back way, that's all.'

'Like a terrorist or something,' she said brushing herself off. There were grass seeds in her hair; he didn't dare reach over and brush them out for her.

'Merry Christmas,' he murmured.

'Hmm.'

Lockie looked at the grass seeds in her hair. No, he couldn't resist. He reached out and touched her head. She flinched.

'What are you doing now?' she said irritably.

'You got something in your hair. Here – '

And that was it. He couldn't help it. He kissed her on the forehead. Whoosh! Aaargh! His toes curled up, his ears caught fire; his knees popped out of their sockets and came back like yo-yos.

Dot looked at him, startled.

'What was that?'

'Um, a kiss?'

'Oh. Okay.'

'I really like you, Dot.'

'Yeah?' She smiled. Oh, it killed him; it made his teeth hurt.

'Well, yeah.'

Dot smiled again and looked at her feet. Great feet, too.

They just stood there, not saying anything. I mean, what can you talk about at moments like this? The football scores? The average rainfall of Guatemala? Michael Jackon's plastic surgery?

They said nothing.

Not a thing.

And then Dot stuck out her hand and grabbed his and squeezed it and smiled again.

'Aw, puke,' said Phillip with his head out the bedroom window.

Lockie and Dot jumped.

'Lovers,' said Phillip disgustedly, wrinkling his nose like the ten-year-old he was. 'Can't you do that somewhere else?'

'Phillip, pull your head in or I'll pull it off,' said Lockie, shaky with anger.

'Did you get your Chrissie present, Dotty?'

'Phillip!'

'It cost fifteen bucks! I can do subtraction, you know.'

'Think about Phillip minus head, then,' said Lockie, preparing to lunge.

'You left that?' said Dot. 'I thought some

95

homeless person had slept on the verandah, like it was their belongings or . . . ' her voice trailed off as she realized what she was saying. 'I . . . oh, geez, I didn't mean . . . I mean it was really nice of you to – '

'Doesn't matter,' said Lockie, absolutely shrivelling in shame and embarrassment. 'It was a kind of . . . joke. It was . . . I guess . . . '

He just couldn't stand there any longer. Lockie slunk off inside leaving Dot out there in the yard, and locked himself in the toilet. He wanted to crawl into the septic tank and live there forever. He wanted to disappear from the face of the earth and not be remembered, not even in the fashion capitals of the world.

THE COUNT OF
MONTE CRISTO

Long after Dot and everyone went home, Lockie stayed barricaded in the toilet. It got dark, but he stayed. The family got stuck into the Christmas leftovers and he stayed. Phillip needed a pee, but Lockie stayed and he heard his brother doing it off the back step. 'The Simpsons' came on the TV, but Lockie stayed and read old *Women's Weekly*s and *Police Gazette*s. He wasn't coming out for anything; he was in there for the long run, for the term of his natural life. Yep, it was the dunny for him, forever and ever, Amen.

At eight-thirty Mrs Leonard whacked on the door.

'Lockie? Blob's pooped her nappy. I need to get in.'

Lockie didn't make a sound.

'What's the problem?'

' . . . '

'Come on, love, I've got a nappy full of pumpkin soup here. Are you sick?'

' . . . '

'Tell you what, I'll just shove it under the door and let you scrape it out for me, huh?'

A vile, life-threatening terrorist device slid silently across the floor of the toilet. Lockie stared in horror. Half a kilo of milk-fed goop wrapped in a pink diaper. Septic fallout! The stink was like a harbour of your very own. It steamed and throbbed like a half-formed alien. Around the edges there was overflow. Yes, it was like pluto-nium pumpkin soup alright, and here and there it had croutons of lino in it. Aaaarghhhh!

Lockie Leonard came out like a man shot from a cannon.

'Ah,' said the Sarge over his book of Lithuanian poems. 'The Count of Monte Christo returns!'

Lockie lay on his bed. The TV was still going out there. The Sarge was doing the ironing and his mum was writing something on the kitchen table. Blob was asleep and Phillip was busy turning the toaster into a blender on the loungeroom floor.

Lockie lay back feeling deeply sorry for himself. Being thirteen was plain hard work. Teenagers should get a humiliation allowance from the government. His love life was a joke, his best friend wouldn't talk to him and everything stank sky high.

Mrs Leonard came in, a bunch of papers in one hand.

'We're having a vigil outside the phosphate works tomorrow night.'

'What?'

'A few of us are taking some action about the harbour.'

'Who?'

'John, Cleve, Queenie, some people from the Fishermen's Association – Merv and Pat Mason.'

Lockie squirmed. 'Great.'

'Just thought I'd let you know. You know, on the off-chance you're still interested.'

Lockie shrugged. 'Uh-huh.'

Mrs Leonard sighed and went out. Lockie rolled over and got his pillow in a half-nelson and pounded it mercilessly against the wall. They were hijacking his protest! Was nothing sacred? Aaarghhh!

LOCKIE LEONARD'S FAMOUS
SHARKPROOF SWIMMING MACHINE

All night Lockie lay awake with the noise of ten million frogs washing over him. They sounded like the Hell's Angels on steroids out there in the swamp, but it wasn't only that keeping him awake. He just couldn't turn his mind off and relax.

Across the room, Phillip ground his teeth mechanically and let out machine gun bursts of snoring.

Lockie counted sheep. He counted frogs.

He wanted to see Dot, real bad.

But he thought about Egg; it got to him every

100

time he rolled over, the sight of poor Egg bawling out there in his mum's shed. Geez, some people had *real* problems on their hands and here he was moaning about some stupid tee-shirt and a bit of embarrassment. What was wrong with his brain? Hadn't he learnt anything at all in thirteen years?

Just on dawn, as Lockie was finally dropping off, Phillip climbed into bed with him without his PJ's on. Lockie didn't have to ask; he knew what it meant. Phillip had wet the bed again.

Lockie got up and left the dry bed to Phillip who was asleep again already. He dressed himself and slipped out the window. The frogs, exhausted from their partying, were silent as he cut his way across the swamp toward Egg's place.

Lockie tapped at the window. The curtain was drawn back and through the flyscreen he could see Egg sprawled asleep, his mouth open, his pimples mellow in the dim light.

'Egg? Oi, Egg!'

With a start, Egg sat up. When he saw it was Lockie, he grunted and lay back on the pillow.

'You orright?' whispered Lockie.

Egg shrugged.

'I couldn't sleep,' said Lockie.

'I was doing orright, myself.'

'Sorry.'

101

'They sacked my dad,' said Egg.

'Oh, mate.'

'On Christmas Day, they sack the minister.'

Lockie leaned against the sill. So that's what all the arguing was about yesterday.

'I don't think they'll stay married after this,' said Egg. 'That'll make the church happy.'

'Let's go to the beach,' said Lockie. 'Let's just forget everything for a moment and just nick off to the beach. That's what I do when everything goes to poop.'

'Lockie, I can't swim, remember?'

'I'll teach you, no problem.'

'Sounds incredibly tempting, Lock. I'll forget about misery for a day and get into terror. You're a bright bloke.'

'It's just water, Egg.'

'It's what's in the water that bothers me.'

Lockie stood back a moment, defeated. He looked along the graveyard of steel that was the Eggleston's yard, and an idea splattered against his brain like a meat pie against a blackboard.

'I'm a genius!' said Lockie.

'Yeah, and I'm Tom Cruise.'

No one who saw those two on the beach that day ever forgot the sight of Lockie Leonard's shark-proof swimming machine. It was pretty low-tech – actually the horse and cart was probably space-age compared to it – but everyone agreed that it was dead original.

From the jetty all the way round to the surf break Egg flapped and spluttered, laughing like a madman's parrot while Lockie steered him best he could. Egg's beachwear was pretty phenomenal – a pair of black Stubbies, a Bonds tee-shirt the colour of baby poo, and some Pinke Zinke on his nose that smelt like pile ointment. On top of the water all you could see was the huge bunch of old fishermen's buoys and cordial bottles that kept him from sinking like the national economy, but under the surface the real business cruised along like a U-boat. Lockie Leonard's famous sharkproof swimming machine was actually the aluminium tubs of two old washing machines joined together with fencing wire. The ends were hacked off and Egg's head and arms stuck out one end and his feet the other so he could kick and flap all he liked. Any shark with the IQ of a fingernail could have burrowed in one end and eaten his way to the other, but Egg felt safe as houses. He felt like Grant Kenny, like Shane Gould, like Marine Boy, even, and Lockie kept telling him he was the new human torpedo.

Little bubbles poured from the tiny holes in the tubs all around him. The floats clacked together and bobbed madly above him and he chugged along ridiculously well. They laughed themselves sick and then made the big mistake of trying it as the Lockie Leonard sharkproof bodysurfing machine. It was Egg's first surfing experience, and it didn't make a convert of him. He looked like one of those guys going over Niagara Falls in a barrel, and he rolled all the way up to the high tide mark before Lockie could pull him out.

'Hm, what's this?' said Lockie. 'A message in a bottle?'

'Am I alive?' said Egg.

'I think that's the spin dry cycle.'

They just lay on the beach and laughed themselves blind. Lockie felt so happy he nearly busted his boardshorts.

BLAST FROM THE PAST

Lockie and Egg, limp with laughing, were strapping the contraption back on the bike trailer when Lockie saw a familiar silhouette on the next dune. His heart hit the pause button and he stared. She was coming their way. Cut off jeans, a Midnight Oil tee-shirt, all that frizzy hair blowing in the wind.

'Uh-oh,' said Egg, his pimples suddenly going neon underneath their zinc paste.

'Battle stations,' said Lockie weakly.

'G'day, Lockie,' she said, smiling nervously.

Vicki Streeton. His old girlfriend. The first girl

he ever loved. The absolute home-baked-economy-sized-discount-final-offer love of his life. Aaaarghhh!

'I saw your gizmo,' she said, pulling the hair out of her eyes. 'It's a scream. Still the torpedo, huh?'

'It was Egg inside,' said Lockie. 'This is Egg. Egg this is – '

'Yeah, I know,' said Egg.

'Are you Tomorrow or the Day After?'

'Geez, word gets around.'

'I just wanted to let you know I'll be at the protest tonight.'

'Protest?' said Egg.

'Ah, the protest, that's great,' said Lockie shoving his elbow halfway through Egg's kidneys. 'That's really great.'

'My dad says the mayor is seriously shat-off about it, though.'

'Yeah?' Lockie scratched his armpit and felt his lone zit vibrate.

'I'm gonna bring some friends, okay?'

'Absolutely,' said Lockie with his heart in slow-mo.

'I hear you've got a girlfriend,' she said looking at her feet. Great feet. The same excellent feet.

'Well . . . '

'He's lost his mind,' said Egg.

'I hear she's a hot grommet. Better than you, maybe.'

106

'And she's twelve this year,' said Egg with a grin.

Vickie's face opened up in a great smile. 'Really?'

Lockie stood on Egg's foot and ground it into the sand. The breeze blew his hair in his face and he was glad of the cover.

'He's a bit of a dirty old man, our Lockie,' said Egg, ignoring him.

'Well, I hope she appreciates him, Egg,' said Vicki. 'Seeyaz tonight, then.'

She walked off, all denim butt and windblown hair and Lockie started stuffing Egg back into the swimming machine where he belonged for the rest of his life.

'Ah, nausea of the heart!' laughed Egg. 'He's suffering apocalyptic hormone disease!'

THE REALLY NICE BOY

When Lockie and Egg got back to the Leonard house in the middle of its slow-fermenting government swamp, there were people everywhere, mostly oldies they didn't recognize. They were all busy cutting cardboard and stapling and painting, and no one looked up at them as they walked through the house to the kitchen. Lockie headed for the fridge; he was so hungry he could have eaten the bottom out of a birdcage. Even his mum's low-fat skim-milk hi-fibre, low-cholesterol zero-sugar totally flavourless and unpleasant rice flour treats. Mrs Leonard was at the kitchen table talking earnestly to a woman with a ring through her nose. Geez, his mum was getting radical!

'Hi, Mum,' he said, burrowing in the fridge for something Blob hadn't already gnawed on.

Mrs Leonard looked up a moment and went on talking.

'Hey, Mum, I'm home. Is there anything else to eat?'

'Excuse us, will you?' Mrs Leonard said to Ringnose. The other lady got up and went out.

'Where the hell have you been?' Mrs Leonard asked.

Egg fidgeted at the edge of the room.

'Down the beach,' said Lockie.

'Since dawn?'

'More or less.'

'With Egg?'

'Yeah.'

'Hullo, Egg,' she said.

'Um, hullo Mrs Leonard.'

'When's the do?' asked Lockie.

'The protest? I didn't know you were still interested.'

'Mum – '

'Don't go mumming me! I've had people here all day. The town smells like, like, like – '

'Pus?' said Egg.

'Yes, pus will do just fine, thank you Egg. The town is smelling like . . . pus and people are coming here because of your noble handbills, and I'm having to deal with it because you can't finish anything you start. You come home raving and moaning about the harbour and get us all razzed up and then call us hypocrites because we're too busy to help and then we make time to help and then you fade off like the Ghost Who Walks. And here I am with a baby and a husband doing double shifts and a kid going back to wetting the bed and a houseful of people who want to do something about the world they live in and YOU'RE AT THE BEACH! It's love again, isn't it? As soon as you get the . . . the . . . the . . . HOTS for a girl you drift off. I can't believe you can let this happen twice, Lockie. You become someone else. You forget your family, your friends, your principles, even. The human torpedo misses the target and the point, do you understand me? Lockie, I'm ashamed of you!'

Lockie closed the fridge. Geez, his ears were on fire. Whew, that hurt. He didn't know where to look. His whole body shrivelled with embarrassment. In front of his best friend! It seemed like the perfect time to head for his room, slam the door in a major way and swan dive onto the bed.

'Um, Mrs Leonard,' said Egg carefully. 'Maybe I can explain.'

'I thought you were genuine, too, Egg. I'm disappointed.'

110

'Geez, Mum, go easy, willya?'

'I'm sick of going easy!'

'Mrs Leonard, Lockie spent the day trying to cheer me up.'

'Oh? And do you need special cheering up today, Egg?'

'Mum, his dad got the sack yesterday.'

'On Christmas Day?'

'Mum, things aren't real good round Egg's place at the moment.'

'I was kind of shrieking interior maximus.'

'I beg your pardon?'

'Kind of upset, you know.'

'He gets depressed, Mum. Geez!'

'Anyway, Lockie was trying to cheer me up. He's been a drongo lately and I was seriously less than happy about his miserable level of achievement in the friendship zone of his life, but today he was trying to suck up to me and cheer me up.'

'Well,' said Mrs Leonard sitting down tiredly. 'Did it work?'

'He tried to drown me. It was fun.'

'Fun?'

'Well, I've been thinking about drasticality, you know. Having someone try to drown you sort of takes your mind off it.'

Lockie clutched his head. 'Nice work, Egg. That *really* clears it up.'

'He's basically a nice kid, Mrs Leonard. You

should be glad to have him. Could be worse – you could have got me. I've got zits and hammer toes and I get depressed. Plus I'm into Death Metal which is a worry.'

'There's nothing wrong with *you*, Egg,' Mrs Leonard said kindly.

'Lockie's just confused, Mrs Leonard. He's having female trouble.'

'Egg,' said Lockie, exasperated. 'Females get female trouble.'

'Oh.'

'I've got – '

'What have you got, Lockie?' asked Mrs Leonard, sniffing a real good heart-to-heart coming on.

'I've gotta go and make up some placards,' said Lockie bolting from the room.

Egg shrugged. 'He's so sensitive, too. Isn't that nice?'

MISTER MEDIA

Being the human torpedo, Lockie got to the protest late, but the sun was still up and the driveway out the front of the phosphate factory had a football atmosphere to it. There were only about twenty people or so down there but they sounded like a vast, wild partying mob. Blurring white everywhere, placards shook and lunged all over. There was chanting and cheering. He saw his mum with Blob in the stroller. There was John East and his friends Queenie and Cleve, all lunging it out in front of the chain-link fence.

As he wheeled down the hill a van overtook

him and he recognized the logo on the side. *Great South TV*. Man, this was going ballistic!

'Whaddawewant?'

'Clean up!'

'Whennawewannit?'

'Now!"

That was his mum with the loud hailer! This was hot!

Lockie unstrapped his placard and joined the circus.

'Better late than forever,' said Egg, grinning.

Egg looked happier than Lockie had ever seen him and a second later he saw why. Egg's dad was with him and shouting like mad till his glasses fogged up.

'Whaddawewant?'

'Cleanup!'

'Whennawewannit?'

'Now!'

Lockie laughed and held up his placard: MEGA POO THANX TO YOU.

'Oh, nice work, Lock.'

'It was all I could think of at the last minute. Show us yours.'

SLIME IS A CRIME, said Egg's.

'Pretty deep, huh?' said Mr Eggleston.

'Sorry to hear about your job,' said Lockie nervously.

'Thanks. Anyway, it lets me join the riff-raff for a day, huh?'

'Oh yeah, you're serious riff-raff, Dad,' said Egg.

Lockie grinned. Mate, this was great. This was like the French Revolution meets the AFL Grand Final. TV cameras started scooting in around them. A woman with aluminium-looking hair traipsed around with a microphone. Lockie saw Vickie and smiled like Liberace's piano. Blokes in suits were at the gate now, telling them to sod off, and why didn't they go and get a job and were they all escapees from the loony bin.

> SAVE OUR HARBOUR
> TWO YEARS TOO LATE
> CLEAN UP NOW
> THE STINK STARTS HERE

There were placards everywhere, and hands clapping and a bit of jostling and gate rattling. John East worked his way over to Lockie.

'Your mum's a real demon on this stuff,' said John East.

'Absolutely,' said Lockie proudly.

'They reckon the mayor's going to show.'

'Really?'

'He's a nasty piece of work, Queenie reckons. It'll be interesting.'

'You've got nice friends,' said Lockie.

'Well, you're biased,' East said with a laugh. 'Just go careful, mate, orright?'

'I don't get what you – '

'Just don't make it awkward for me, okay?'

'Sure,' said Lockie, still not getting his drift. 'No worries.'

Just then someone shouted, 'Cops!'

A paddy wagon wound down the hill and behind it a black BMW.

'Pustling!' A woman called.

'Excellent insult,' said Lockie.

'That's his name, dorkoff. The mayor.'

'Pustling?' That wasn't a name; it was a skin disease, surely.

The aluminium hairspray head with mike ran out to meet the BMW and the blokes humping the videocams followed. The chubby little guy was talking even as he got out of the car. Lockie saw the cop car pull up and a skinny constable got out and then the Sarge. The Sarge waved to people in the crowd; he doffed his cap and smiled. He was like Jack Nicholson arriving at an airport. Lockie half expected him to start signing autographs. Oh, shame and agony! Couldn't his old man have been an accountant or something?

'This is a complete beat-up!' shouted Mr Pustling at the cameras. 'These people are the kind we should be very wary of. They frighten people for the sake of it.'

'What about the EPA report two years ago, Mr Pustling? Has the town done a single thing to clean up the harbour?'

'These people want to close down a good

116

business and put a lot of decent hardworking people out of a job. And I won't stand for that!'

'Sir, what about the terrible smell?'

'We live by the sea. It has an odour sometimes. What do you want, Chanel No. 5?'

'Do you eat fish from the harbour?'

'Every day. Nothing wrong with it.'

'Do you swim in it?'

'Every day. What a tourist asset it is. These people are dragging this town's good name through the mud.'

'He's a liar!' someone yelled.

The reporter whirled and stuck the microphone in Queenie's face.

'What do you think, madam?'

'Des Pustling is a liar and a thug and the reason this town stinks is because the people who run these factories are frightened of him.'

Lockie's jaw dropped. Suddenly the reporter shoved the mike near his gaping mouth.

'What about you?'

'Me?' he squeaked.

'Do you want to see this plant closed down?'

'Ah, um – '

'What about these people's jobs?'

'Er – '

Death! Aaargh! Total annihilation and shame!

'We don't want the factory closed down at all,' said Egg.

'And what's your name?'

117

'Axl Rose,' said Egg with a dumb smirk.

'Go ahead, Axl.'

'Well, we don't wanna see any people lose their jobs – besides the mayor – but the phosphate plant and the mill over there and all the industries with stuff going into the harbour have to clean up their act.'

'Shut up, pizza face!' yelled Pustling bustling in towards Egg. 'I'll have you in – '

Just then the Sarge bolted in and got between the mayor and the crowd.

'See? See?' Pustling screamed at the cameras. 'I need protection from this mob. This is a riot!'

'Well, actually,' said the Sarge apologetically, 'it wasn't you I was protecting, sir. But go ahead, don't let me interrupt.'

The mayor went pink, then white, then blue and turned and headed for his car. The crowd cheered. Lockie tried to cheer with them but inside he felt like a wet Kleenex. Everyone had been so cool and he'd been like a total stumblebum and in a couple of hours the world would know. Lockie Leonard, Mister Media. Not!

Lockie Cracks a Sad

The loungeroom was crowded with celebrating, excited, expectant people and Lockie stayed in his room. He could smell the pizzas and the boxes of Kentucky Fried Chicken doing the rounds. He heard the Sarge come in from his shift. He heard Phillip telling everyone his stupendously boring knock-knock jokes. Lockie just lay there unable to celebrate.

A knock at the window. It was Egg.

'Why are you cracking a sad?'

'I'm not,' said Lockie.

Egg climbed in through the window and sat

119

on the chest of drawers.

'Did you see my dad there? Man, I couldn't believe it! He said he had nothing to lose and he was glad.'

Lockie smiled weakly. 'I didn't see you afterwards.'

'Well, you took off like a cut cat. Anyway, I just walked home with Vicki.'

'Vicki Streeton?'

'Yeah. She's not so bad, you know.'

'Uh-huh?' Lockie felt cold all of a sudden. Vicki? And Egg?

'I sort of guessed you'd go home with Dot.'

'Dot wasn't even there,' said Lockie.

'Yeah, she was sitting in her oldies' Land Rover; didn't you see her? Didn't get out the whole time.'

Lockie munched on his lower lip. That was pretty disappointing. Maybe she was sick; maybe he should have looked for her. And maybe she didn't give a rat's ring about Angelus Harbour. After all, she didn't live here.

There was a roar from the loungeroom.

'Let's go and see it on the news,' said Egg. 'Mate, we gave 'em heaps today.'

'Nah, you go.'

'Come on, Lockie, don't be a squid.'

Egg hauled him up and shunted him out the door. They walked into the steam of food and talk and suddenly there it was on the idiot-box. A whirl of faces and slogans. Everyone cheered at a shot

120

of Blob with two fingers up her nose. Vicki Streeton shouting. Mister Eggleston beaming. Queenie with a fist up. Then Lockie's agonizing, squirming five seconds of death and then Egg giving them plenty – 'We don't wanna see any people lose their jobs – besides the mayor.'

'Axl Rose, eh?' someone yelled over the TV.

Lockie slipped away, leaving Egg to cop the glory. He kicked the screen door open and saw Dot standing by the clothes hoist in the last of the light. He hesitated a moment and then trudged over.

'Hi,' said Dot.

'You didn't see me go down in flames on TV. You really missed something.'

Dot shrugged.

'What's up?' he asked.

'I'm bored, I guess.'

'With what?'

'This town, this holiday. The swell's gone. It's just dead here.'

Lockie swung thoughtfully on the clothesline. 'Geez, I thought it was a pretty action-packed day.'

'For you, maybe.'

'Egg said you stayed in the car at the factory.'

'So?'

Lockie dropped to the grass. 'Your oldies are really into the environment. Your mum's famous for it. I just – '

'That's their thing. It's got nothing to do with

me. I just wanna go surfing.'

'What happens when the crap in the harbour pukes out onto the beaches? You won't be able to surf in that.'

'I don't live here, Lockie. It's not my problem. This is my summer holiday.'

It was dark now and Lockie couldn't see her. She was just someone talking in a cloud of mosquitoes. It was like he was talking to someone he didn't know at all. Geez, he was so confused, and numb. He wanted to shout at her. Didn't she know every problem was everyone's problem? Didn't she care about things like this? What was all this sulking crap, all this moaning about the surf and 'my summer holiday'? Man, it was so childish!

But he didn't yell at her. He was too depressed, and besides he wasn't so perfect himself lately. Face it, she was hardly twelve years old. What did she know any different? Hell, she probably surfed all day and went home to watch Disney videos and play Barbie and Ken in her room.

'You didn't come and see me today,' she said.

'I had something I had to do.'

'You went to the beach with Egg.'

'Yeah. He's having a real bad time in his life, you know. He's my best friend and – '

'Here, I brought this back.'

Lockie saw a pale flash in the dark and felt a brush of cotton against his face. The tee-shirt.

122

'What d'you mean?'

'I'm giving it back.'

'You didn't like it.'

'It's okay.'

'Geez, thanks, Dot.'

'I just don't like competition.'

Lockie balled the tee-shirt up in his hands. Mosquitoes were giving him intravenous hell but he just stood there and took it.

'No, you love competition, Dot. I bet you'll end up Women's World Champ. You'll be famous one day.'

'I don't mean that kind of competition.'

'I know,' Lockie said taking the tee-shirt and heading straight inside without her. He heard her leaving, crunching up the gravel drive. Oh, man, he told himself, that was the shortest romance on record. You broke all previous on that one, son. The average cold lasts longer than this. He'd had longer nosebleeds, seen longer mini series on the telly. And now Egg was walking home with Vicki? There is no justice out there. Man, what a day.

He lay on his bed and laughed. He just couldn't help himself. He didn't see the face at the window because he pulled the tee-shirt over his streaming eyes and smelt the coconut smell of Dot Cookson and laughed till his teeth hurt.

LEPERS

Egg and Lockie walked down the main street to buy a paper and see how the campaign was progressing. The pong off the harbour was truly astounding. In the sunlight the water was dark green and thick as soup.

'You look terrible,' said Egg.

'She dumped me,' said Lockie with his arms hanging off him like wet washing.

'Dot? Dumped you? It never got going, did it?'

'You're probably right. Well, I was in deep, mate.' Lockie kicked at a Coke can and missed completely. On top of everything else, love was making him a bit unco.

'Up to your nostrils, mate.'

'Well, it didn't work out. We're incomp . . . incomp . . . '

'Incompatible?'

'Absolutely. And mate, she's eleven and three quarters. What was I having – a midlife crisis?'

Egg had something dead clever to say but suddenly they were surrounded and the thought vanished. Lockie hit the pavement first. His head whomped like a split melon and then Egg crashed down beside him. Five faces peered down at them.

'It's you two, innit?' said a guy with a tattoo of Marcia Brady on his left cheek. 'On the telly, it's you two smart turds.'

'Yesterday and the Day Before.'

Lockie tried to spit out his tongue and speak but a Blundstone boot pressed into his throat.

'Our dads and our uncles and aunties and brothers and cousins – '

'I think he means his family,' said Egg who copped a backhander for his trouble.

'They work at the plant, see. It's their jobs. They been there since – '

'The dawn of time?' offered Egg. He got a thump in the guts for that one, and shut up.

'They like their jobs, orright? So we want you two little snots to go back to your hippy mates and call off the noise, orright?'

'It's not about jobs,' stammered Lockie.

'What would you know, kid? You never had a job.'

'I make my bed and wash the Falcon on Saturdays,' said Lockie.

'Oh, mate, I'm impressed.'

'We just want the outlet cleaned up,' said Lockie. 'The plant doesn't have to close down.'

'Get your facts straight, kid. Read the paper. Change your tune, 'cause we know who you are.'

Then they were gone and Lockie and Egg lay on the path out in front of the post office like two banana skins, getting their breath back.

'You orright, Egg?'

'Yeah. I think we better buy a paper.'

When they limped into the newsagent's there was a mob of headbangers and bogans crowded around the music and motorbike shelves. One was reading *Tattoo Monthly*, another had *Thrash and Throttle*, a third opened *More Metal* and moved his lips carefully as he read.

'G'day,' said Egg.

None of them would even look at him. 'Noddy, Dork, Dishrag, how's things?'

Nothing, not even a hello.

'I'm starting to feel like a leper in this town,' whispered Egg.

Lockie bought a copy of the *Angelus Advocate*

126

and straight away he saw the problem.

BUSINESS PULLS OUT OF ANGELUS, said the headline.

Management of the Great South Phosphate and Fertilizer plant and the Angelus Textile Mill said yesterday that it was ready to shut down operations in Angelus after harassment by agitators and eco-groups calling for a halt to their activity. This would mean the loss of two hundred jobs and a vast industrial investment in this town . . .

He didn't bother to read on; he passed it to Egg and they slipped out of the shop into the stinky street.

'This is totally sputumnal,' said Egg.

They walked in a daze down to the town jetty and stared out at the hideous poison green of the harbour. A few kids from school were catching blowfish out on the end, letting the ugly little things puff up and then splatting them with their heels. It was a heartwarming sight. The kids froze when they saw Lockie and Egg.

'Here come the Big Men,' someone muttered.

'Show-offs.'

'Suckholes.'

'Well, g'day to you too,' said Egg.

'I can't believe youse two,' said Rabbit Reed, a pasty Year Eight who thought he was Prince in a pink skin. 'You think it's cool to go round having protests and doing all this GREEN stuff. People are sick of it. They're sick of Bob Geldof and Sting and the Oils. Mate, that phase is past. You look so sad and desperate out there, trying to be cool. You're a joke, the both of you.'

'We're not doing it to sell records,' said Egg.

'No, you think it'll get you chicks.'

'Rabbit, you're sick.'

'Look at the water,' said Lockie. 'Smell it. That's why we're doing it. Frankly I'd rather be surfing than getting my head kicked in. What happens when this cack gets out of the harbour and onto the beaches? We're not gonna stop just cause people think it's uncool.'

Lockie gave up and walked off and Egg went with him.

'I can't believe it,' said Lockie.

'Don't worry,' muttered Egg. 'I know for a fact that he's into Michael Jackson.'

'Oh,' said Lockie with a laugh. 'Now *that* is sad.'

'People are just hard to figure out.'

They nursed their bruises back up through town and headed home.

Mrs Leonard dabbed some horrible smelling stuff on Egg's face and chest.

'That'll do you,' she said kindly.

'Oh, no,' said Lockie, 'He wants more, Mum. He loves that smell.'

'Thanks, Mrs Leonard.'

'Maybe you two should stay home for a few days,' she said. 'This thing has really blown up. I'm copping a bit of badmouth myself.'

'Who from?'

'Oh, coppers' wives, people in the street.'

'Geez, Mum. I thought people would just see the point and get behind us.'

'It turns out Mr Pustling – the mayor – owns part of the phosphate factory and some of the wool-mill. He owns the dredges in the harbour and the whole town is terrified of him. He's just too powerful. They'd rather lose the harbour than risk getting offside with him.'

'It's like . . . like *The Godfather*,' said Egg.

'Looks like we're out of our league,' said Mrs Leonard.

'Maybe I better go home,' said Egg. 'I promised I'd help Mum and Dad pack.'

'You're not leaving town are you?' said Lockie, alarmed. They'd just become mates. He couldn't leave now!

'I dunno yet. I think they're trying to decide.'

'I'll help,' said Lockie, getting up all fidgety and eager.

'No, maybe it's better if you don't. Things are pretty tense at home just now.'

'Okay,' said Lockie, a bit hurt. 'Seeya then.' He leaned against the door jamb and rubbed his chin against his arm as Egg went off down the drive. He whacked his knuckles against the wooden frame and winced.

PARENTS

Lockie headed for John East's on his creaking bike. He needed advice and plenty of it. John was a Guidance Officer after all, and Lockie was finally ready for some major Guidance. Life was just too complicated! I mean, why didn't they give you a map and a compass when you were born so you could find your way around?

He wanted to talk about Egg.

Then there was Dot – man, his heart was aching.

And this Des Pustling routine.

Lockie's brain felt like a roasted cashew.

He couldn't believe the sight that awaited him. There he was, the hairiest man in living memory out the front with a lawn mower and a machete. The jungle was tumbling before him. He hacked and pushed and tore and grunted and sweat ran off him like creeks through a rainforest. But when he looked up and saw Lockie, he snuffed the mower and threw down the machete.

'I s'pose you've come to explain it all to me,' said John East ominously.

Lockie's smile did a quick evacuation. 'Um, pardon?' He climbed off his rusty crate and leant it against the letterbox.

'No doubt it'll all be a terrible mistake. I'm getting sick of schoolkids, Lockie. I don't know why I bother. I thought I made myself pretty plain yesterday about you and Dot.'

Lockie just stood there. He was a couple of kicks behind the play.

'I don't get it,' he said.

'Do you see a Land Rover in my driveway?'

'No.'

'Does that suggest anything to you, Leonard?'

Leonard? Wow, this was like school already. John East was fit for an explosion.

'Did they go shopping?'

'No, Lockie, they went home. A week early, they went home. My friends. My visitors. They pulled the pin. This morning.'

'Oh, man,' said Lockie, sitting on a pile of wet,

hacked grass. 'But why?'

John East gritted his teeth. 'Don't fool with me, Lockie. Don't play funny buggers!'

'Sir, are you on drugs?'

'You're a smart alec, Lockie.'

'I'm sorry. I just wondered. I honestly don't get this. Honest to God, I don't know.'

John East walked over to his front step and sat down.

'We really needed their experience,' said Lockie. 'Egg and I don't know what to do next.'

'Shut up, Lockie.'

Lockie shut up.

'They're my best friends, and I think you just cost me that friendship.'

Lockie's jaw dropped with a thunk against his chest. 'Sir?'

'What happened with you and Dot?'

A little squeak came out of Lockie's throat.

'For all I know, they've gone to the police.'

The police? Lockie's ears popped. His hair did Mexican waves. His eyes shrank in his head.

'Did you – '

'Sir?'

'I mean did you.'

'Sssir?'

'You know what I'm asking you.'

'Sssss?'

'Relations. Did you have . . . relations with Dot?'

'Sssssspphhh?'

'I mean, you see yourself as pretty . . . advanced.'

Advanced? Him? Lockie? The slow motion replay himself? He wondered when he'd just burst right here like a party balloon. Pop! End of story.

'Lockie, you have to tell me. Take a deep breath; you're going all blue. Lockie?'

'I liked her, sir,' he squeezed out, sounding horribly like Whacko Jacko himself.

'Okay. Right, okay.'

'I bought her a tee-shirt for Christmas.'

'Yes. Hmm.'

'I saw her down the beach twice.'

'Alright. You're doing fine, Lockie.'

'That's it, sir.'

'Now, don't be devious.'

'I swear, sir, that's it.'

'Come on, Lockie, be a man. Own up. What happened last night? She came home in tears.'

'She did?' Lockie cheered up at this. She actually cried? She gave him the flick and then cried? Man, that was love. 'Really?'

'All night. Queenie nearly went to the police. But then she realized that your dad *is* the police.'

'He's only one of 'em, sir.'

'What happened, Lockie?'

'She gave me back the tee-shirt.'

'Was it suggestive?'

'Sir, you've got a dirty mind!'

'Alright, she gave you back the tee-shirt. Then what?'

'She said she was bored with the holiday and her oldies. She was sulking. The protest, I guess. She was mad because I spent the day with Egg.'

John East. 'That's all? That is ALL?'

'You know me, sir. I don't lie. I'm too lazy . . . Did she tell them something else had happened?'

'Well, no, not . . . no.'

'Oh, man . . . '

'Tell me straight, Lockie. How far did it . . . get?'

'Sir, I'm a gentleman.'

'You could be a sore gentleman.'

Lockie got up off the grass and brushed himself off. 'I kissed her on the forehead. Once. That's it. I mean, she's a whole year younger than me, sir. It's so embarrassing!'

John East tugged at his beard. 'Embarrassing, yeah, I think that covers it pretty much. You wanna cup of tea?'

'No thanks. I think I'll go home and recover.'

Lockie climbed on his bike.

'Lockie?'

'Sir.'

'Sorry about the grilling.'

Lockie shrugged. 'Parents, sir. They worry.'

'I'll call 'em tonight.'

'Say hi from me.'

'Are you serious?'

'No, sir.'

Lockie rode off smiling.

Return to Sender

But the relief wore off and the facts didn't. A girl he liked was gone for good. His campaign against pollution looked sick. And his best friend was home packing, maybe leaving town.

Lockie wandered through the reeds and boggy ground outside his place. He watched tadpoles shoot like bullets across the drainage ditch. It looked like he was on his own again. At the end of the year he was back where he began it – lonely. Nothing seemed to last.

Phillip joined him by the ditch. He had a bat and ball in his hands.

'Sorry about the thing with Dot,' he said.

'That's okay, Phillip. You're just immature. It's not your fault.'

'Actually, I was jealous. Dot was a spunk.'

Lockie turned and looked at Phillip. 'Good grief. You're ten years old!'

Phillip shrugged. 'Anyway, there's plenty more fish in the sea.'

'I'm not hearing this.'

'You wanna hit?'

Lockie sighed and had a few hits with his playboy brother who called girls 'babes' and still wet the bed. Life just cracked him up.

That night on the news the unions came out against the 'environmentalists' and said the protest threatened jobs and should be called off. Workers carried their own placards outside the gates of the phosphate plant and the wool-mill and the message was the same.

The Leonards sat glumly at the dinner table.

'Well, I s'pose mussels and crabs just aren't cute,' said the Sarge. 'Shame there's no dolphins or koalas to defend.'

'We'll never get support with the unions against us,' said Mrs Leonard.

'Can't we get the mayor somehow?' said Lockie with a mouthful of mashed spud.

'He'd do to you what you're doing to that

spud,' said the Sarge.

Blob gnawed the laminex off her high chair and spat little chips of it onto the table as if to illustrate the point.

'You have to get the unions on your side.'

Lockie chewed dejectedly. This was all beyond him; he was seriously out of his depth.

'And the only way to get them interested is to . . . well, affect their lives.'

Lockie stared at the Sarge. You could tell he'd just had an idea because his ears glowed red as stop lights.

'Sarge?'

'But I can't have anything to do with this,' he murmured.

The Sarge got up and yawned theatrically and slumped on the sofa. 'So what I'm about to say is just me talking in my sleep, orright?'

'Are you okay, love?' said Mrs Leonard.

'Just bushed, that's all. Hmm, sleepy, sleepy. Hmm . . . '

Lockie left the table and sat on the floor next to the sofa. The Sarge lay back smiling, eyes closed.

'Now the union sees what comes out that pipe as someone else's problem . . . and what goes on inside the plant and the mill is their problem.'

Lockie squinted. Maybe the old fella really was out to it.

'You have to make them the same problem. People have to see consequences now and then.

A matter of return to sender, address unknown . . . '

And then the Sarge slipped into crooning this old dorky song, one those doo-wop jobs, and then he really did fall asleep. Maybe.

Lockie looked up at his mum. She shrugged.

'It's the shift work,' said Phillip. 'And the poetry he reads. He just wants to be interesting.'

Oh, he's interesting alright, thought Lockie, trying to figure it out.

KER-AAAAAASH! PHHT! PHHT! BOINGGGGG! Halfway through 'Neighbours' it hit him. Lockie understood. Return to sender! Yes. Most absolutely indeed! My father is a genius, he thought.

'Mum?'

'Hmm?'

'Can I go over to Egg's?'

'It's late.'

'I know, but it's real important.'

She looked at him. He was quivering like a little dog about to pee on the carpet.

'One hour. Exactly.'

'Mum, you're . . . you're . . . '

'That's fifty-nine minutes and counting.'

Lockie was gone.

Lockie knocked on the window. Egg poked his head out glumly.

'Hi.'

'I've got it.'

'You won Lotto.'

'Don't be sarcastic.'

'Sorry,' said Egg. 'Don't mind me. I'm just having my life turned upside down. I'm just moving house. I'm just waiting for my oldies to call it quits. Don't mind me at all.'

'Orright, more sarcasm – you're entitled to it. Listen does your mum have any secret desire to be liked by people?'

Egg squinched his face up, wondering. 'Not that I've noticed.'

'What about an artistic thing . . . you know, recognition?'

'Well, that yeah. She wants people to think of her as Michaelangelo with an oxy torch, you know.'

'The Ninja Turtle?'

'No, you dropkick, the painter.'

'We have to talk to her.'

'You're insane, Lockie.'

'I need a win, mate.'

'We all need a win now and then, but – '

'Look out, I'm coming in!'

In he went, the human torpedo, bringing the curtains down and the Egglestons running.

The door crashed open.

'Hi,' said Lockie. 'Mr and Mrs Eggleston, I need to talk to you.'

'I believe you,' said Mr Eggleston rubbing his eyes under his specs.

OPERATION CONSTIPATION

All next day Lockie watched Mrs Eggleston do her stuff. She wasn't the kind of person you met every day. She was really intense and didn't bother with small talk, and she wasn't actually that friendly, come to think of it, but she really seemed to know what she was doing with an oxy torch. The morning was a blur of blue sparks. Egg and Mr Eggleston sat on the back step, the packing forgotten. They just watched with Lockie.

She lined up eight old diesel drums and welded them together four and four. On top of them she bolted a couple of pine pallets, and then she made

143

a frame big enough to hold an oxy set.

'Will it float?' asked Lockie.

'It'll float,' Mrs Eggleston said. 'It'll take me and the set and a few bits of steel.'

Lockie looked at Egg and saw that he was beaming.

'You'll need a second kayak,' said Mr Eggleston. 'To help steer it and stabilize it.'

Mrs Eggleston looked at him. 'You're right.'

'Me? Right?'

'Don't go on. You're right. I'll do another kayak.'

'Have we got time?' said Lockie, nervous now.

'What time's low tide?'

'Eight-twenty-six tonight,' said Lockie.

'No problem,' said Mrs Eggleston, and at that precise moment she smiled. It was such a rare sight everyone looked away embarrassed.

'I really appreciate it, Mrs Eggleston,' said Lockie. 'We all do.'

She shrugged in her overalls and flipped her mask back into place. 'Egg asked me,' she said, muffled by the glass. 'And . . . my husband.'

'You're a genius,' said Lockie.

'Yes, probably.'

'I'll be back at seven, Egg. Mr Eggleston, can you back a trailer?'

Egg's dad squirmed and blushed. 'Well, not that well, actually.'

'You'll be fine.' Then Lockie thought of the

second kayak. They needed another person. 'See you at seven.'

'Operation what?' the Sarge whispered over the enquiries desk at the police station.

'Constipation,' said Lockie with a jittery grin. 'As in . . . return to sender, address unknown.'

'Uh-huh.'

Lockie looked around at the Wanted posters and the Reward posters. This place always made him nervous. It stank of blokes. Cigarette smoke, boot polish, and large blokes.

'We just need the trailer for a couple of hours. Mr Eggleston will drive.'

'I hope he drives better than he preaches.'

'You mean yes?'

'Just go very quietly, orright? Gawd, the things I say in me sleep.'

Lockie ran the old Hoover up and down the house till it got asthma. He dusted, he polished, he did the dishes and helped hang out the washing.

'Why do I get the feeling you're sucking up to me, Lockie?' said Mrs Leonard.

'Cause I am,' he smiled.

'Okay, spit it out.'

'Can you paddle a canoe?'

'Is this one of Phillip's dirty – '

'No, honest. I need someone who can use a kayak.'

'What for?'

Lockie pegged out one of Blob's nappies. She ate so much linoleum that the patterns were starting to come out in her nappies. He looked at the floral pattern in wonder.

'A commando operation,' he said.

'Are you on drugs?'

'Mum – '

'I'm gonna ring your father.'

'He already knows.'

'Oh my God.'

'Mum, it's an operation!'

'You're sick? Lockie, why didn't you tell me?' Mrs Leonard spat out a mouthful of pegs and got him in a bear hug. 'Oh, Lockie, young people just don't communicate!'

'Mum, I'm not sick!'

'You're not?'

'But thanks for the hug.'

And then he told her about tonight and she smiled like a cat that got the low fat, low cholesterol, high calcium cream.

'Constipate? Life is one long toilet joke for males.'

Lockie nodded. 'I guess. Can you do it?'

'I can't. I'd love to, but I can't. I've got Blob and Phillip to look after. What about Mr Eggleston?'

'We need him in the car.'

'Try John East. He'll help. He's hairy, but he's nice.'

'Mum, you're a genius!'

She nodded. 'In my dreams.'

Lockie leaped into the saddle of his ancient bike and went flat out for John East's.

But there was no one home. He couldn't believe it. The yard was mowed flat and boring as any other joint in the street and no one was home.

He peeled out of the yard and headed for the beach. Maybe John was having a surf. But there was no swell and hardly anyone on the beach with the onshore blowing hard.

He couldn't chase all over town for him; he needed to think of someone else.

His brain hurt. Mate, it glowed hot and smelt of burning rubber. He couldn't think of anyone. Phillip was too small and didn't swim so great. The Sarge was on his shift till midnight. Maybe someone from school? But he didn't really trust anyone. No one understood him at school, not even when he was Mister Popular with . . . with . . .

There *was* someone.

The one other person who understood him. The one kid who knew what was going on in the harbour.

Lockie headed for a phone box and hoped he had thirty cents tucked away somewhere in his shorts.

'Hello?'

'Um, arh . . . '

'Yes, who is it?'

'Listen, I know you said I should never call and everything but – '

'Lockie?'

'And I don't mean to invade your personal space and everything – '

'Lockie, is that you?'

'But I really need some help.'

'Lockie?'

'Vicki?'

'What help?'

Lockie's heart skittered around like a cat on a glass coffee table. The last time he made a call like this he was getting the big shove, the chop, the axe, the elbow, the big A. It wasn't a nice memory. He shouldn't be doing this. His heart was only just glued back together and then there was Dot giving him the flick only hours ago. How much rejection can you take in one life?

'Um, can you use a kayak?'

'Is your name Lachlan Robert Louis Stevenson Leonard?'

Lockie laughed. Operation Constipation was on the trot.

A MAJOR STUFF-UP

It turned out Mr Eggleston was a worse backer-upper than anyone believed possible. Down in the swampy bushland below the industrial end of the harbour, he pointed the trailer at the stinking water and ended up with it in the bush every time. Mrs Eggleston started to hiss like one of her cylinders and Egg put his face in his hands.

'What about we just drag the pontoon off and haul it to the water?' said Vicki.

'Good idea,' said Mr Eggleston wiping the sweat from his glasses.

Lockie could smell that old vanilla scent. Vicki

Streeton. Her elbow against his, her knee against his shaking leg.

'This whole thing better work,' he said nervously.

'Oh well,' said Egg. 'Win or lose, it's better than watching "Neighbours" on the telly.'

Dragging an eight tank pontoon across gravel and reeds and broken bottles had seemed like a good idea at the time. Lockie felt he knew what those poor Egyptian slaves went through to build the pyramids. He'd seen those Charlton Heston movies – he knew his history. And this was taking a century.

'Even "Neighbours" is more fun than this,' giggled Mr Eggleston.

'Going to the dentist is more fun than this,' said Egg. 'Going to school, even. Getting needles in the bum . . . anything.'

But they got it to the water in the end and it floated merrily on the puky low tide.

'Okay, let's get the kayaks,' said Egg.

'I'll get the oxy,' said Mrs Eggleston.

'I'll hide the car,' said Mr Eggleston.

'Just don't try to back it, Dad,' said Egg.

'Nine-thirty, Mr E,' said Lockie.

'Righto.'

151

Lockie was so relieved to share his kayak with Vicki instead of Mrs Eggleston that he hardly noticed the vile smell of the water beneath him. The full moon lit their way and cormorants croaked out in the channel. In the strange light he saw Vicki's hair blowing in front of him. She leant against the pontoon and steered it on. It was a weird looking craft out there, bouncing between the two kayaks. It thunked against them, blunt and graceless. It handled like a Woolworths trolley on a sloping footpath.

'Careful,' whispered Egg, 'You'll tip us over!'

'Keep it off with your paddle,' said Lockie.

'Whew!' said Vicki. 'I hope you can swim in this stuff. It's getting worse.'

On they went zig-zagging across the shallows with the raft bobbing and writhing toward the high reeds.

'Where are we?' called Mrs Eggleston.

'Straight ahead,' said Lockie. 'Get behind it now and just push.'

With a horrible scraping noise the drums crashed into the sharp reeds and they plunged into the shadowy rustling mess ahead until they heard the sound of pouring water and their eyes began to burn.

'This is it,' said Lockie.

Egg switched on the torch. The outflow pipe stood high and dry, pouring gunk out onto the creeping algae that covered the sandy bottom.

'It's concrete!' hissed Mrs Eggleston. 'I can't weld concrete!'

'The last bit's metal, Mum,' said Egg. 'Look, thirty centimetres.'

'Oh. I thought it was a stain.'

Lockie's heart started up again.

'Go for it, Mrs Eggleston.'

From up the hill near the phosphate plant you could see a strange flickering light down near the water, as though some kids were cooking crabs on a fire. Though why anyone would go crabbing down in that nobody knew. The Supervisor high in his glass box looked curiously, watching the sputtering light. It looked like fireworks. Actually, he decided, it was quite pretty. Was that someone bending down there near the perimeter fence? The Supervisor didn't get to figure that one out just yet because two blokes were belting up the stairs screaming blue murder.

Lockie tried not to look directly at the blue burning light of the sparks, but he could see the cap firmly in place now, with only the tiniest dribble seeping out the seams. The whole pipe was welded shut.

'Brilliant!' said Egg. 'Let 'em work that out with a pencil!'

Mrs Eggleston went around plugging it up,

touching the weld up here and there and Lockie looked up at the yellow lights of the plant.

'What'll happen?' asked Vicki, wiping her eyes on her windcheater.

'Maybe nothing,' said Lockie. 'But all this stuff comes from up there, and if it can't get out down here, it's gotta go somewhere. Like a blocked toilet.'

The oxy torch went out.

'That's it.'

'How long will it take?' said Mrs Eggleston, flipping her lid back.

'Dunno,' said Lockie. 'Maybe hours.'

Suddenly a siren went off up the hill.

'Cops!'

'No,' said Lockie. 'Look!'

Orange lights flashed in the windows of the phosphate plant. A horn went off and the yellow lights dimmed and flickered.

'Lockie,' said Vicki, 'you're a genius!'

'No, I'm just good at stuffing things up, I guess.'

They hit the water and paddled till their blisters had blisters.

Up on the hill it was goop city already. It was deeply unpleasant. It was like changing a nappy the size of the Starship *Enterprise*.

Whew, you could smell it from here.

A Major Weirdness

The next day, with the town going totally ballistic, Lockie rode up to Egg's place feeling unreal. He hung a wheelstand most of the way up the hill and the wind ripped through his hair. On the corners he leant out like Wayne Gardner; he defied death and gravel rash – he felt invincible. Down in the harbour there were five strikes and fifty TV cameras. People said 'Sixty Minutes' and 'Hinch' were there and guys from Greenpeace, and the sleepy old government. Man, it was like a food fight in a phone box!

Lockie cornered madly into Egg's street and

saw the removal van and the bum fell out of his day. Blokes were humping boxes and chairs and stuff into the truck and Egg was out there on the verandah with his CD amping severe noise into the neighbourhood.

Slowly, miserably, Lockie walked into that zone of grunge and unhappiness. Egg looked up, smiled weakly, and turned the Motorhead down.

'You got another house in town, right?' said Lockie.

Egg shook his head. 'Perth. Back to the city.'

'Oh, mate.'

'Yeah.'

'Oh, man.'

'Yeah.'

Lockie kicked his bike in the guts and rust sprayed everywhere. 'It's . . . it's just not fair!'

'Dad said there just wasn't any alternative in this town. He's right, I guess. At least they're not splitting up as well. I mean, it could be worse.'

Lockie sat down, totally trashed inside. 'Yeah, I'm sorry. That's good.'

'I think last night really helped them.'

'Last night? How?'

Egg shrugged. 'I dunno. Marriage is like that. Weird, eh?'

'Weird, yeah.'

Lockie put his chin on his knees. He felt like someone had died. He would rather have the harbour stink and still have his best mate, but somehow he couldn't say it. His eyes burned and he didn't know where to look.

'What are you like at writing letters?' asked Egg.

'Rotten.'

'I guess there's the holidays.'

'Yeah.'

There were so many things he wanted to tell Egg, so many things to thank him for and apologize for and remind him of. This was worse than getting the flick from a girl. This was like drowning.

'We really gave 'em heaps last night,' said Egg.

Lockie nodded.

Egg cranked up the CD and the street choked with the pumping, thrashing blast of Motorhead and they didn't need to say anything at all. Birds scattered everywhere and dogs howled. It was wicked and most uplifting.

STREET THEATRE

For a week, Lockie didn't get out of bed. Mrs Leonard and the Sarge didn't mind so much – at least they had the use of the toilet this time – but they tried to hook him out every day with news about the dredging and the stuff in the news about the mayor's rotten deals. He just stayed there, though, stinking up the room with his unwashed blokey smell that even Phillip noticed after a while. The frogs did their wild thing out in the swamp. Blob came in and ate his bedspread to cheer him up. Phillip made Lego cars for him and tried to get him interested in the undie ads in the *Women's Weekly*, but nothing worked.

Lockie felt dead inside.

He was left behind.

There was no one anymore.

He was deceased, zero, nothing.

Lockie got close to the point of drasticality. His surfboard got cobwebs. His mum ironed his wetsuit by accident and hung it in his wardrobe, and he didn't care.

On Friday a letter came.

Dear Lockie,

I'm sorry about all the trouble with John and everything. I was being dumb. I was jealous! I didn't mean to give you a hard time.

Sincerely,

Dot.

P.S. I still think you are a spunk.

P.P.S. Can I have my shirt back?

Lockie stuck it back in the envelope and wrote RETURN TO SENDER on the front. But he didn't mail it yet; not yet.

On Saturday, the Sarge got restless. His patience ran out. He came into Lockie's room cap in hand.

'Lockie, the swell's up. I mean it's quite . . . quite large.'

Lockie nodded.

'I think you should go surfing. I know there's not many times when a parent needs to suggest this, but I definitely feel you should hit the beach. You're getting boring, son.'

Lockie blinked.

That did it. The Sarge was out of there. Lockie heard him start the Falcon. He heard the clunk of the trailer on the towball.

'Mrs Leonard! Phillip?'

A rumble of footsteps through the house. They burst into his room and lifted the bed, hoisted the whole thing up with him in it and clunked it through the house and out into the yard and dumped in on the trailer.

'Get the board, Phillip.'

'I'll get the wetty,' said Mrs Leonard.

Lockie lay there stunned as his father lashed him securely to the trailer with the tow rope. Phillip slid the board in beside him and his Mum tucked the wetsuit under the half gnawed bedspread.

'This won't take long,' said the Sarge.

Lockie actually tried to tough it out. He didn't know why because the smell of the sea was so inviting and people were really seriously staring at him parked in his bed on a trailer in the middle of a crowded carpark. It wasn't just polite staring, it was denture-dropping stuff, shrieking, pointing, awful public display stuff, but he thought he could hold out. The Sarge cacked himself, sitting in the Falcon, reading *Jane Eyre* or something. Lockie believed he was up to it. He'd been through worse, he'd cut the mustard.

But he caught sight of someone familiar out of the corner of his eye and his hair went mental. It wasn't possible! He couldn't be that unlucky! He saw a smile, a glint of braces, and he reached for the wetsuit. He was sort of half in and half out of it when she rocked up. Geez, it was like history repeating itself!

'What's this, then?' said Vicki. 'Street theatre?'

'Kind of,' said Lockie, with his pyjama sleeve sticking out of his wetty sleeve and his head caught between buttons and zip.

'You gave 'em heaps, Lockie. You did good.'

He tried to shrug, but the logistics were against him.

'I heard about Egg leaving. It's a bummer. I liked him.'

'Me too.'

'And that twelve-year-old surfie chick, I heard about that, too.'

'You did?'

Vicki smiled. Her hair blew back off her face. 'Well, I won't hold it against you. In the future, I mean.'

'The future?'

'Yeah. You know, tomorrow and the day after?'

Lockie swallowed.

'Anyway, you better get out of here; you're causing a scene. Seeya later.'

'Yeah,' said Lockie. 'In the future.'

The swell was long and clean, and it wound into the bay with a tired roar on the sand bar. Lockie paddled stiffly and felt the cool water zing against his face. He sat and swivelled quickly and dug hard into the water as the great lumbering peak rose behind him. Down the long glassy hallway of the wave he fell, turning and cranking and crouching low. His knees knocked with the force of it. He streaked for the tiny almond eye of daylight at the end of the tube with the growl of the ocean all around him, and from the beach you could hear the sound of the human torpedo crashing through into daylight:

YEEEEEEEEEEEEE – HAAAAAAAAAAAAAAAAA!

ALSO BY TIM WINTON

LOCKIE LEONARD – HUMAN TORPEDO

Lockie Leonard, hot surf-rat, is in love. The human torpedo is barely settled into his new school, and already he's got a girl on his mind. And not just any girl: it has to be Vicki Streeton, the smartest, prettiest, richest girl in class.

What chance have you got when your dad's a cop, your mum's a frighteningly understanding parent, your brother wets the bed and the teachers take an instant dislike to you and then you fall in love at twelve-and-three-quarter years old? It can only mean trouble, worry, mega-embarrassment and some wild, wild times.

An ALA Best Book for Young Adults

' . . . a story about sexual awakening and morality; about standing on your principles or ignoring them to belong to the group.'

Scott Johnson, The *Examiner*

AVAILABLE FROM PENGUIN BOOKS

ALSO BY TIM WINTON

LOCKIE LEONARD – LEGEND

Lockie Leonard's survived the worst year on record. His first year of high school, settling into a new town, his first mad love affair – it's all behind him. He's about to turn fourteen and things are looking up.

But the world of weirdness hasn't finished with him yet. His little brother's hormones have kicked in and that's not a pretty sight. His lino-munching baby sister refuses to walk or talk. His dad starts arresting farm animals for a hobby and his poor mum suddenly won't stop crying. Right in the middle of this family shambles, an old flame comes scorching back into his life. Ouch!

OKAY, WHAT GIVES?
PLEASE EXPLAIN.

As his whole world goes down the gurgler, Lockie discovers things are never as simple as they seem. Not even for grommets.

AVAILABLE FROM PAN MACMILLAN